PRAISE FOR JENNI JAMES

Beauty and the Beast
(Faerie Tale Collection)

"Jenni James takes this well loved faerie tale and gives it a paranormal twist. Very well written and hard to put down, even on my cruise vacation where I had plenty to do. Looking forward to others in Jenni's Faerie Tale series. A great escape!"

—*Amazon reviewer, 5-star review*

Pride & Popularity
(The Jane Austen Diaries)

"This book was unputdownable. I highly recommend it to any fan of Jane Austen, young or old. Impatiently awaiting the rest of the series."

—*Jenny Ellis, Librarian and*
J..ica

"Havi...nit
retellings ....
that Pride  is my top choice and receives my highest recommendation! In my opinion, it is the most plausible, accessible, and well-crafted YA version of Pride and Prejudice I have read! I

can hardly wait to read the [next] installment in this series!"

"I started reading Pride and Popularity and couldn't put it down! I stayed up until 1:30 in the morning to finish. I've never been happier to lose sleep. I was still happy this morning. You can't help but be happy when reading this feel good book. Thank you Jenni for the fun night!"

Northanger Alibi
(The Jane Austen Diaries)

"Twilight obsessed teens (and their moms) will relate to Claire's longing for the fantastical but will be surprised when they find the hero is even better than a vampire or werewolf. Hilarious, fun and romantic!"

"Stephenie Meyer meets Jane Austen in this humorous, romantic tale of a girl on a mission to find her very own Edward Cullen. I didn't want it to end!"

"We often speak of Jane Austen's satiric wit, her social commentary, her invention of the domestic novel. But Jenni James, in this delicious retelling of Northanger Abbey, casts new light on Austen's genius in portraying relationships and the foibles of human nature--in this case, the projection of our literary fantasies onto our daily experience."

—*M.M. Bennetts, author of May 1812*

Prince Tennyson

"After reading Prince Tennyson, your heart will be warmed, tears will be shed, and loved ones will be more appreciated. Jenni James has written a story that will make you believe in miracles and tender mercies from above."

—*Sheila Staley, Book Reviewer & Writer*

"Divinely inspired, beautifully written—a must read!"

—*Gerald D. Benally,*
author of Premonition (2013)

"Prince Tennyson is a sweet story that will put tears in your eyes and hope in your heart at the same time."

—*Author Shanti Krishnamurty*

The Frog Prince

Jenni James

StoneHouse Ink 2013
Boise ID 83713
http://www.stonehouseink.net

First eBook Edition: 2013
First Paperback Edition: 2013

ISBN: 978-1-62482-076-2

Cover design by Phatpuppy Art
Layout design by Ross Burck – rossburck@gmail.com

This book was professionally edited by Tristi Pinkston
http://www.tristipinkstonediting.blogspot.com

Published in the United States of America

This book is dedicated to Tanner,
my green boy. I love you.

The Frog Prince

Chapter One

HIS ROYAL HIGHNESS PRINCE Nolan turned to his mother, Queen Bethany of Hollene Court, and announced, "I have decided to do it!" He threw the missive from his intended, Princess Blythe McKenna, upon the small end table near the settee in the formal drawing room where his mother preferred to take her tea.

"You decided to do what, dear?" his mother asked as she sipped at her cup.

"I have decided to visit Blythe in disguise." He sighed and sat down across from her in a green-and-white-striped overstuffed chair. "I must meet her in person.

I cannot ascertain from her letters what she is truly like. It is a great muddle, and it is time I decided once and for all if I will indeed offer my hand or not."

"But you are already promised to each other!" She set her cup upon the saucer and placed them both on the end table. "What is this nonsense?"

"Mother, it is not nonsense. Betrothing me as an infant is not something I can accept, especially when I am quite unsure whether my bride-to-be is a spoiled child or a blessed saint."

She gasped. "Nolan! Watch your tongue." She never did enjoy his mention of saints as general cant.

Nolan sighed. "Forgive me. But there is something so self-possessed about her letters that quite causes me to scowl. I have got to sort this out for myself before any royal announcements are made. It is time I approached this differently, visited her as an uninvited guest, and saw how she would treat me."

"My goodness!" The queen's hand flew to her prominent bosom, the plum ruffles of her gown doing much to make her appear rounder and plumper than she actually was. "What do you plan to do, Nolan? Disguise yourself as a pauper or some such?" She looked truly scandalized.

He chuckled to himself. Perhaps it was the mischief-maker in him, or perhaps he enjoyed unsettling her feathers, but whatever the reason, he took pleasure in watching his mother's reactions. At times they were simply invaluable. "No, not a pauper. I have decided to take it a step further than that."

"How shall you disguise yourself, then?"

"Perhaps ... as an animal?"

"I beg your pardon?" Her arms swung out, one violently upsetting the tea things upon the end table so they came crashing down upon the floor and shattering. One fragment skittered across the marble flooring to nudge his shiny boot. Normally his mother would be aghast at the mess and insist it be cleaned immediately. However, this time it was as if she did not know it had happened. "Why in all the great heavens would you decide to take on the form of some animal? You, Prince Nolan! One of the handsomest men who has ever walked the halls of this great court—you now wish to present yourself to your betrothed as an ... an ..." Her voice trickled off as she began to sway.

"Mother, do not swoon. It does not become you," he said languidly as he slowly leaned forward, ready to assist if need be.

Bethany sat up. "I do not swoon! I have never swooned."

"Just so."

"But why must you appear as an animal? What will they think of us? Nolan, this cannot be right. You must consider a less ludicrous scheme."

He laughed. "No. It is perfect—how else will I be able to learn what this girl is really like? If I come to her dashing and princely, she will no doubt be quite smitten, as they all are. But if I come to her as, say, a dog or something, she is bound to show her true character."

"A dog! My son, a *dog*. I cannot bear it. I cannot even think such a thing. It is not the right animal at all!"

"Perhaps you are correct." He thought about it for a few moments. "A dog might be a little too easy. Far too many people love dogs."

"Well, it is good to know you are finally speaking some sense!"

"No, I must plan on something much more hideous."

"More hideous? Nolan!"

He folded his arms. "Yes, something all girls detest and run screaming from."

"You would not dare! This is all some hoax, is it not? You are merely jesting your mother, like you and Sariah did when you were children, constantly pulling those maddening pranks upon me. Tell me this is one of your larks. Tell me."

"I am afraid not, Mother." He stood and walked toward her.

"Then why? I do not understand," she said. "What are your plans? Will you simply put on a costume, or—"

He leaned down and kissed her cheek. "No. I will not wear a costume. I plan to ask the village herb woman to put a charm over me."

"Nolan!"

"Not for long, perhaps thirty days or

so. But I need to know for myself if Blythe is indeed the woman of my dreams, or if my instincts are correct and she will prove to be more of a handful than I am willing to take on."

"But you cannot back out of your betrothal now!" the queen exclaimed.

"I cannot back out of anything that I was not asked to be a part of. The design was yours and Queen Mary Elizabeth's, not mine." When she gasped once more, he quickly added, "I promise not to break anything off hastily. I will wait the full thirty days before doing so."

"Nolan, you are out of your wits!"

"No, Mother, I feel for the first time in my life that I am finally doing something especially intelligent. If Princess Blythe can prove me wrong and is indeed the woman I desire, she will want for nothing in all the land. I intend to treat my wife with the utmost of courtesy and devote all my life to creating a magical existence with her. However, she must pass this small test first, because as spoiled as she seems to be, it is better to know that I would indeed be marrying a princess and not a harpy!"

"Nolan, I will never, ever understand you as long as I live."

"Good." He grinned. "Then my work here is done."

His mother paused before saying, "Do you mean to tell me that you shall turn yourself into an animal for thirty days?"

"Yes, precisely."

"And you will look just like this animal."

"Yes."

"And poor Blythe McKenna has thirty days to treat you kindly, and then once she does, you will turn back into a prince and offer your hand to her?"

"Hmm … I do see some flaws there." He sat back down upon the striped chair. "Perhaps if she does something sooner that would prove her kind heart—perhaps I would have the charm bring me back to my princely form earlier."

Bethany shook her head as if he were completely foolish. "What would you have her do?"

All at once Nolan smiled. "I have it! Princess Blythe must kiss me!"

"Kiss an animal?" She fluttered her hand. "You are mad!"

"Oh, I hope so. This will only be entertaining if I do have some touch of madness in me." He winked.

"My word." She sighed. "What animal have you decided to become?"

"The most revolting, un-kiss-worthy creature I can think of."

"And that is?"

"A frog." He chuckled at her appalled face. "Yes, I shall be a frog prince."

Chapter Two

PRINCESS BLYTHE RUSHED BAREFOOT along the crooked stream, dodging daffodils and tulip shoots as her feet sank into the lush grass, until she came to a beautiful pond near the castle. She spread the skirts of her blue gown and settled upon her favorite boulder. This was by far her most preferred spot on the palace grounds. Here she could lean back and stare up at the lazy clouds as they floated past, or roll over on her stomach and swirl her fingers in the clear water.

She would sit out here in the sunshine for hours, dreaming and escaping castle life. This was where all her plans for the future were made. This was where she truly had time to herself and no one would irritate her.

On most days, she would bring with her the large faceted crystal ball that had been the center drop piece of their family's chandelier in the main throne room. When the great light fixture crashed to the ground a few years back and most of the crystal was broken, her mother had decided to toss the whole thing.

Thank goodness Blythe had been walking by when she heard the fall or she would have never seen the pretty ball rolling on the floor. Nor would she have been able to snatch it up and bring it out here to the pond to play with.

She held the ball up and allowed the sunshine to filter through its many facets, painting rainbows all over her gown and the boulder where she sat. It was so stunning. When she was excessively bored, she would place the ball up to her eye and look out into the world, seeing hundreds of little reflections blinking back at her. This time, however, she tossed the pretty crystal up into the sky and caught it.

There was something so very calming about doing just that—throwing the ball up and then catching it. She leaned back and tossed it again and again and again. As she tossed, she thought, allowing the rhythm of the soaring ball to soothe her whirling mind.

Why did she have to get married to a prince she did not even know, let alone like? Well, to be honest, she had never met him before, so therefore could not judge him too harshly, but goodness! With such a face as his portraits showed him to have, how could he not be the most inane buffoon who ever lived?

True, he was handsome—remarkably so. She sighed. That was probably the worst thing about Prince Nolan—his features. Why, if he were plain, or had more common looks, perhaps she would not be so critical of him. But how could she ever take a man with such striking looks seriously? He must be a complete braggart.

She stopped tossing the ball and pulled his latest missive from her pocket. After staring at it a moment, she crumbled the thing up. She had never read such idiocy in her life! The topics of his conversation were clearly meant to be delivered to a completely dim-witted female, someone who would properly "ooh" and "ah" over such manly exploits like his latest hunting kills and marksmanship with the longbow.

She rolled her eyes. As if she cared one whit about the number of times he had bested this ogre or that ogre. Where was the wooing? Where were the sheets of music he had written for her, songs she could pick out on her pianoforte and think of him? Where were the bouquets delivered to her door? Where were the poems and attributes to her person?

Bah!

She crumpled the letter around a small rock and tossed it into the pond. With satisfaction, she watched it slowly sink beneath her view.

"A man as self-centered as that can stay beneath the waters of the pond where he belongs. I will not marry such a man. I *cannot* marry such a man—it is beneath my principles. I have waited my whole life for this man to truly see me and love me, and yet, it will never happen." She sighed and muttered to herself, "Nay, he will only ever think of himself. I must have more than that. I must."

She glanced toward the castle, where the happy shouts of her two elder brothers met her ears as they returned from their ride. Looking up at the fourth-story windows, she knew her two younger sisters were dutifully working away with their governess, doing their schooling and excitedly chattering about whatever it is ten- and eleven-year-old girls chatter about.

Blythe sighed again. How she abhorred her age!

With her brothers nineteen and twenty, it made her mere seventeen quite unbearable.

How she longed for a friend, or a sibling her own age. How she longed not to always be forgotten and alone.

She looked at the spot where she had thrown Prince Nolan's letter and pressed her lips together. It would seem that another person destined to be in her life would not see her. He did not even care to know her. Not once did he ask her questions—only arrogantly going off about his own accomplishments. Did he not wish to know who she was at all?

Tucking her arm beneath her head, she blinked up at the clouds and sighed once more.

Good heavens, she was in a melancholy mood. If she were not careful, she might find herself in tears and that would never do. She blinked again.

But what if, what if she truly was that— oh, goodness! There were some days when she had to wonder if she was even worth getting to know. Mayhap her thoughts and ideals and dreams and all those things she longed for and loved—all of it—perhaps they were too simple for handsome princes to care about. Maybe if she did open up and share her wishes and secrets, he would lose all interest in her. Clearly there was a reason why she was the forgotten one of the family.

Perhaps it had nothing to do with age at all and was simply because she was that worthless.

Urgh.

Blythe sat up quickly and dashed at her tears. Enough. This was silliness to the extreme, and such thoughts were unacceptable on beautiful, sunshiny days. Wallowing in self-pity was only warranted on rainy, dismal days—today was too perfect.

She tossed her crystal up in the air. There.

Just seeing it go up already calmed her.
Grinning, she watched as it soared higher, its
facets glinting with multi-colored rainbows
as it winked in the sunlight before traveling
back down to her waiting hands. This time,
however, it would seem she had thrown it
much harder than usual, for it bounced right
out of her palm and splashed some six feet
away from her into the pond.

"Oh, no!" She scrambled to her knees
and peered over the edge of the boulder into
the water. She could not even make a thing
out! It was just her luck—the ball *would* have
fallen right into the deepest part of the pond.
Even if she did risk her mother's wrath by
going into the water and ruining her gown, she
would never be able to see the bottom anyway,
and therefore never be able to fetch the ball
through the soft silt and rocks. The crystal
would be gone forever! No, no, no.

Urgh. Her frustration doubled, and she
felt like weeping out of her stupidity alone. It
would seem she was not worth much beyond
the typical dim-witted female who would
love a smug prince. That letter was clearly
addressed to her, for who else would be so

mindless as to toss their favorite ball into the pond?

Closing her eyes, she brushed angrily at the tears that were much too close to the surface today.

"Would you like some help?" asked a male voice Blythe had never heard before.

Her eyes snapped open. She looked around the empty pond and out toward the shrubs and trees surrounding it. "Hello?" she asked. Was she hearing things? That voice sounded so real.

"I am down here," he answered.

She glanced down and shrieked. There, just a few inches from her hand, sat a very large and slimy frog.

Chapter Three

NOLAN JUMPED BACK AT the sound of her shriek. The girl had incredible vocals for one as dainty as she seemed to be. In fact, Princess Blythe looked so much smaller than he imagined, he first thought she was one of her younger sisters—though when he saw her crumple and toss his letter into the pond and mumble that nonsense about him not seeing her, there was no mistaking that she was his intended.

So disgusted was he with her treatment of a note he had written and the wasted journey of his footman in delivering it to her, he had nearly hopped away and gone home right then.

She was the pampered princess he believed her to be.

However, the memory of the night before, stuck out here in the cold, and the thought of making his way several miles back to his castle as a frog, did not appeal. The herb woman had been sure to poof him to this exact pond, telling him that first thing in the morning, Blythe would make her way down to her favorite spot and he could meet her then.

When Nolan initially had this scheme of turning into a frog, he had forgotten the small detail that he would *become a frog*, not just look like one, and therefore find himself a snack for most of the animals out there. In reality, this was probably not the wisest course of action he had ever taken.

Nevertheless, he was where he was, and therefore he would make the best of it. Since the spell would not be complete for another thirty days or until Blythe took pity on him and kissed him, he was more than likely safer here in this pond than becoming someone's supper. He would be even more safe with her—no matter how petulant she turned out to be.

"Calm down," he said to the screaming girl as she scurried off the boulder. "I have come to offer my assistance." Apparently she was even more terrified of frogs than most females. "Did you not lose a fine crystal ball just a few moments ago?"

Blythe stopped screeching long enough to stare at him. "What did you say?"

"Did your ball fall into the pond?"

"You are speaking in coherent sentences."

"I would hope so!" He puffed out his chest, forgetting for a moment the state he was in. "Royalty is usually taught how to speak properly as a child."

"Royalty?"

Drat. Why did he have such a dimwitted noggin? Now how would he explain this? The charm did not forbid him from saying who he was, but he had hoped to keep his identity a secret. He cleared his throat, deciding it was best not to lie too much. "Yes, I am a prince."

"You?" Blythe laughed annoyingly. "There are princes in the frog kingdom?"

He sighed. "There is only one prince that I am aware of—and he is me."

Schooling her features, she asked, "You

honestly believe you are a prince?"

"I do not just believe it—I am."

She took a step forward. "Is that why you can talk?"

"It is one of the reasons, yes." He decided to explain at least the basics. If he did not provide *some* answers, who knew what her imagination would come up with. "I have been enchanted into this state."

"You are under a spell? Are you certain?"

"Yes."

"Then why are you here in my kingdom? How did you get here?" She seemed skeptical. "Should you not be under a spell in your own kingdom?"

"No. I have my reasons for being in this exact spot." However, if he did not distract her soon, he would be revealing much more than he should. He hopped forward a few paces and was pleased to see that she did not move away from the rock. "Nonetheless, I would like to grant your favor now, if you wish. May I collect your ball for you?"

She stepped back as if suddenly remembering the ball. "Yes, please!" She smiled.

Nolan blinked. The girl had a remarkably pretty smile; in fact, he was quite fascinated by it. He could not help but stare and wonder what her mouth would feel like against his. After some seconds of silence, he realized how awkwardly he was behaving and cleared his throat. "I will get the ball—in exchange for something, of course."

Her smile dropped. "Er, what would you like?"

A kiss! "Uh…" He could not simply rush and ask for a kiss this early. Great heavens, he was such a fool. However, he certainly wished for a much better place to sleep tonight than the pond. He searched her features. Would she be kind enough to take him in? *Of course! It is the perfect test!* "I would like to become your guest at the castle."

She did not appear pleased. "I beg your pardon?"

"I will fetch your crystal in exchange for being treated like a guest in your home."

"What exactly would you expect of me?"

Nolan shrugged his froggy shoulders. "Why, nothing more than common courtesy. I am an enchanted prince, and I find the flavor of insects appalling and this pond too cold and damp for my tastes. I would love to be given proper meals and a warm bed to sleep upon in exchange for fetching that precious ball of yours."

"In short, you wish me to treat a frog as well as I would any of my most particular friends?"

"Precisely!" Now they were getting somewhere. "Yes. Treat me as your dearest friend, and I promise you will be rewarded handsomely."

"Are you mad?"

He grinned. Apparently every female he met would think the same. "Quite possibly. Now, have we come to an agreement?"

Blythe looked at the pond and then back at him, her face scrunched in up in disgust. But just when he thought she would say no, she surprised him by replying, "Yes. I promise to do as you ask and treat you as my greatest friend if you would please return my ball to me."

"Done." He bowed his head and then dove off the boulder into the cool, crisp pool.

His eyes adjusted easily to the murky

waters as he swam deeper through the fronds and mossy rocks below. It took a couple of minutes to locate the ball. Its crystal winked at him as the sun suddenly peeked around a cloud and streamed into the pond. It was also a bit of a struggle to collect the thing, removing debris from around it with his webbed feet and then capturing the ball into his wide mouth. Once he had it, he was able to swim easily to the surface and deposit it upon the shore.

"You did it!" Blythe exclaimed as she ran around the boulder and picked up the ball. "I was afraid I would never see it again!"

"Yes. It was a bit of a chore to find it, but—" Nolan halted when he looked up and saw the girl running away, the crystal in her hand. No good-bye, no thought to keep her promise to him. Not even a "thank you" was tossed his way. "It was just as I believed," he muttered. "She is a pampered, spoiled, extremely vexatious monster!"

Chapter Four

BLYTHE MADE IT ALMOST to the castle doors before she remembered her promise to the frog. She had heard the maid's clanging of the triangle while he was underwater and knew her mother would be worried if she did not make it in time for tea. When the frog popped up just then, it was all she could think of—to get home as quickly as possible. So she hastily snatched the ball up and ran to the castle.

It would not have been such a great issue had she been in the rose garden near the south side, like she had told her mother she would be, instead of sneaking off to the pond nearly a

quarter of a mile away. If the queen knew how
many times a day Blythe headed over to the
pond to daydream instead of doing something
practical—like creating bouquets or sewing
on her embroidery or painting watercolors—
she would be livid. Her mother simply hated
the thought of her ruining her gowns by the
muddy water.

As if she had ever damaged a gown—she
was always careful. At least she tried to be.
Blythe looked down and brushed at a few dirty
spots upon her skirts before opening the door.
She felt a momentary stab of guilt at leaving
the frog so suddenly, but honestly, there was
nothing she could do about it now. He would
have to wait until she could make it back down
there after tea.

She scurried to the east drawing room
and nearly collided with her mother. Queen
Mary Elizabeth II scanned her daughter's
countenance and crossed her arms over her
bright pink gown. "Where have you been?"
she asked. "I sent a maid out to search for
you, and she returned saying you were not in
the rose garden like you said you would be.
Now you have shown up completely flushed as

though you have been running."

Blythe debated lying, but quickly dismissed the idea. Her mother was notorious for getting the truth out of her when the occasion arose. "I wandered down to the pond."

"Blythe!" Her mother sighed. "Why? What is so fascinating that you must continuously traipse down to that murky place?"

"It is beautiful, and I feel calmer once I am there."

"Yes, but must you go every week?"

Blythe glanced at her. Did her mother actually believe she only went to the pond once a week? "Yes. I must. I love it as much as you love your embroidery."

The queen clicked her tongue in disapproval before declaring, "Well, at least it allows you exercise. The walk alone is—"

"Is a mere jaunt. A quarter of a mile is nothing."

"In this heat?" Her mother seemed appalled. "If you do not manage to ruin every gown you own with this odd habit of yours, you shall surely develop a great case of the megrims, the way you enjoy gallivanting around in the blazing sunshine."

It took every ounce of control Blythe had not to roll her eyes at her mother. But honestly, did the woman really live in such backwards times as all this? Instead, she smiled politely. "I am sorry."

Her mother huffed. "No, you are not. But never mind that now." She waved her hand and motioned to the tea cart. "Pour us all a cup. Your brothers will be joining us as well."

"Yes, ma'am." Blythe dipped a quick curtsy and walked over to the heavy-laden cart. It was full of the necessary tea items, but also had plates of scones, sandwiches, tarts, and fruit. If she had not heard that her brothers would be coming down, she would have known they were by the cart alone. Cook did like to outdo herself when it came to the princes. She was always telling Blythe how wonderful it was to have such strapping lads about the place to feed, since they would be sure to eat every scrap.

Her brothers were on their summer holiday now, but would soon begin the hunting season and so would head north to the royal lodge to host large hunting parties with their friends in the surrounding areas.

Blythe took a deep breath as she sat down and began to pour the first cup. Why was it that everyone else seemed to have something to do? How she longed to have her own party or adventure to look forward to. But no, every single day was the same—endlessly pouring tea for her mother and whoever happened to join them.

Who cared for tea when she could take a picnic lunch and go to the pond and read a book, or even better—have a real adventure and do something still more fun? She paused as she began to pour the next cup. Though she did have one secret all her own. However, she was not quite sure how much of adventure it was—it was more of a necessity, and it was kept in such concealment that only two of the castle servants knew what she did.

But no, it was not that she longed for. She wished more for an activity to do openly and share with a friend. But what could a mere girl do? Ugh. It was always the men who had all the adventures. Carefully she poured the cup, but then nearly dropped it when her brother Jeremiah burst in the room.

"I am in love! I am in love!" he announced as he walked over to the queen.

"My goodness! What are you on about?" she asked as he gave her cheek a quick kiss.

He plopped onto the settee and grinned. "Love, Mother. You should really learn the meaning of the word. It is simply magical."

"Who are you in love with?" Blythe asked.

"Do not listen to a word Jeremiah says," David said as he came into the room and kissed the queen's cheek as well. "Hello, Mother. Before he sets you in a tizzy, know that he is simply in love with Thunder— nothing more."

"Thunder?" She pulled back.

"Yes, Thunder!" Jeremiah sighed. "Thunder is only the greatest horse that has ever been ridden and I must own him—I must."

David walked over to the tea cart and quickly filled a plate. He winked at Blythe as he took the cup she offered. "Thank you."

"Whoa! You had better not eat it all. I have not had mine yet." Jeremiah jumped up and fetched a dish.

"None of us have," their mother declared. "We have been waiting for you wastrels to show up." She walked over to Blythe. "And if you two snatch every bit before we have our own servings, you will be sent to your rooms without anything to eat at all—and Blythe and I will have a merry feast to ourselves."

Jeremiah groaned and set a few scones back upon the platter. "Well then, hurry up so we can see what you do not want."

Blythe laughed. "Goodness! The way you two act, it is as if you have never eaten anything in your lives before now."

David grinned and opened his mouth to say something just as the butler appeared and announced, "Forgive me, Your Majesty, but there seems to be a strange guest who has come to speak with Princess Blythe. I had thought perhaps you would like to visit with him first, as it does not appear at all the thing for the princess to have such connections."

"Me?" Blythe asked.

"Well, what do you mean? Is there anything untoward about the fellow?" Her mother walked toward the butler.

He opened his mouth and then shut it again. "I do not know how to say this, Your Majesty. But it would appear as though Princess Blythe's caller is a rather unusual talking frog."

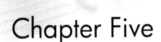

Chapter Five

"A WHAT?" ASKED BLYTHE'S mother. "I beg your pardon—what did you say?"

Blythe set her cup and saucer down and stood up.

The butler cleared his throat. "A talking frog."

"Mother, let me go and speak with him. I know why he is here." Blythe rushed forward and was about to walk out the door.

"Just a moment!" The queen stormed up to her. "What is this nonsense about a frog?"

Jeremiah laughed. "Yes, what type of riff-raff have you been keeping company with?"

"Perhaps she is in love with it." David

grinned.

She could have boxed their ears. "Very humorous."

"Hey, if you are half as in love with the frog as Jeremiah is with the horse, this could be fun. Let us all go and meet him," David said as he sat his plate upon a nearby end table.

"Now this I have to see—little Blythe's gentleman caller." Jeremiah's laughter grew louder as they came toward her.

"You would not dare!" Blythe blocked the doorway. "You will not go and mock him. He came to see me, not you."

"Aye, perhaps she does love him!" Jeremiah whispered loudly behind his hand. "Do you see how defensive she has become?"

David waggled his brows. "He must be quite the looker."

"If you take another step, I will flatten you both!" Blythe glared as her brothers attempted to remove her hands from their vice grip upon the doorframe. "Mother, help me."

"Boys!" the queen chided. "Get your plates and eat your food, or you will be sent back outside to muck the stalls." She turned toward Blythe. "Remove your hands from the door. You may have unusual animal playmates, but kindly do not act like a monkey in this castle." When Blythe lowered her arms to the snickers of her brothers, her mother brushed past her and said, "Come now. We shall meet this toad together."

"He is a frog."

Her mother gave her "the look" as she waited for the butler to lead the way. "Well, thank the heavens! A frog! And here I was worried it was a toad. I am so much more relieved now."

If ever there was a woman who had mastered the art of sarcasm, it was the queen. "He is an enchanted frog," Blythe replied as they began to follow the butler down the long hallway.

"Better and better," her mother mumbled. "Honestly, Blythe, tell me this instant if he is a pet you found at the filthy pond."

"Yes. He is."

"And why did he come? Did you not explain to him that you were not in the habit of entertaining animal callers? Or did you invite him along to try my patience even more?"

"Mother! Must you be so against everything?"

"When it comes to slimy toads coming to speak with my daughter, yes, I will be against it!"

"He is a frog."

"Is there a difference?"

"Well, yes. A toad is at least three times bigger."

Her mother shuddered. "Mercy, do not say another word!"

The butler stopped at the small waiting room near the great hall and swung his arm out. "He is just through here, Your Majesty."

"Thank you," she said as she swept into the room.

Blythe quickly followed to find the frog perched quite respectably upon the blue chair by the window.

"Hello," the queen said as she folded her arms. "My butler has informed me that you can speak. Is this true?"

"Yes," answered the frog.

"So you are enchanted?"

"I am, Your Majesty." He bowed his head.

"And you are here to converse with my

daughter?" They both glanced at Blythe.

"Yes. She has made me a promise and I have come to remind her of it."

Blythe rolled her eyes. This was just wonderful. Things became so much more awkward once one's mother knew about them. Could he not have come in another way and allowed her to keep her pledge secretly so as not to alarm her mother? Already the queen looked as if she were about to explode.

"I beg your pardon—did you say my daughter made you a promise?"

"Yes."

"And when was this?" She placed her hands on her hips. "How well acquainted are you two?"

"We have only just met today."

"And already my daughter has pledged herself to a *frog*?"

Oh, for heaven's sake! "Mother, I did not pledge myself—it is not that type of promise. He did not ask to marry me—my word!"

"Well!" Her mother waved her hand in front of her face like a fan. "Then before I draw too many more false conclusions, could you please explain, in detail, why you have come and are even now sitting upon one of my nice chairs with your pond-soaked bottom?"

His face took on a look of shock. "I am perfectly clean, Your Majesty."

"Just so. Now answer my question before I toss you out on your ear."

He grinned. "I think you mean flippers," he said cheekily as he waved a foot. "I do not have ears."

The queen began to tap her shoe.

"Do not tease Queen Mary Elizabeth," Blythe said. "She is quite serious."

"Or I could always give you over to the cook, if you would prefer." Her mother smiled. "Frog legs are such a delicious treat."

The frog laughed. "Oh, you are much more fun than I anticipated!"

Blythe glanced at her mother and was surprised to see a smile upon her lips.

"Now, speak, toad." The queen raised an eyebrow. "Blythe, you will remain silent. I wish to hear what he has to say."

He cleared his throat. "Well, in exchange for fetching her ball of crystal from the deepest part of pond, the princess promised to allow me to stay here with her in the castle as her special guest. Except once I returned with the ball, she immediately collected it and ran here without me. So I have come to guarantee that she upholds her part of our bargain."

"I see." The queen turned to Blythe—she did not look pleased. "Is this true?"

Blythe glanced at him. "Yes."

"And you could not have promised something else? To treat this frog as a special guest was the best you could come up with?"

"It was the payment he requested. I wanted my ball back and I could not have gotten it without him."

"And if you felt this way, why did you abandon him? A princess should never take promises so lightly."

"I am sorry. I heard the triangle ringing for tea and ran as quickly as I could. I had forgotten about the pledge until I was nearly to the castle." She looked at the frog. "Once I remembered, I planned to come and collect you after tea."

"Tea?" He hopped a bit closer on the chair. "Did you say you came home for tea? I love tea! And I am incredibly famished. Do you perchance have tarts as well?"

"He really is enchanted, is he not?" her mother exclaimed. "For would a simple frog know what tea was?"

"Aye. I am."

"He claims to be a prince," Blythe said.

"A prince?" Her mother stepped closer. "And if you are indeed an enchanted prince, may I ask what kingdom you hail from? And just who are your parents?"

Chapter Six

"NO, YOU MAY NOT. This charm does not allow me to reveal who I truly am," Nolan easily lied.

Blythe's mother put her hands on her hips. "And we are supposed to go on your word only in accepting that you are an enchanted prince?"

"Well, no matter whose name I gave, you would have been going on my word anyhow, since I clearly do not look like my parents."

She huffed. "Very well. What should we call you, then?"

"Uh …" He blinked. "Well, since I cannot tell you my real name, what if Princess Blythe picked a name for me?"

The princess gave him a funny look as if she were trying to figure something out—something besides a new name for him.

"Have I said anything amiss?" he asked.

She brought her head up. "No. Forgive me. I was merely curious about a small matter. A name for you? Hmm …" She tapped her chin as if she were thinking. After a few moments, she said, "Perhaps Caspian?"

The Caspian Sea. A very nice choice for a frog. "I like it very much." He grinned.

"Caspian it is," the queen said. "And how long do you plan on staying?"

"My charm will wear off in thirty days."

"Good heavens!" Blythe exclaimed. "And you mean to stay with us that whole time?"

Her mother sighed and looked at the princess. "Well, I hope receiving that ball was worth this." Then she glanced at him and sighed. "You are welcome to stay as long as you wish. I promise my daughter will treat you with the utmost of respect at all times. And if she does not, you are to inform me of her actions. You are our guest, and I am determined to teach Blythe some responsibility."

"Mother, I have no difficulties in seeing that he is well treated."

"You say that now," she said. "But after a few days, you may find it quite tiresome to always have a frog about, near your plate at the dining table, constantly with you wherever you go, etc."

Blythe looked at him and he smiled a very cheeky froggy smile. She blinked and he chuckled. What he would give to discern what she was thinking. Even though she did not seem overly kind, at the same time she was not as repulsive and rude as he expected her to be. Perhaps it was time to get to know her a bit more.

"Never mind all of this." The queen waved her hand and abruptly turned from the room. "We can discuss this over tea before it becomes cold. Let us remove ourselves and eat. I am famished, and the poor toad is ravenous as well," she said as she walked out.

Blythe glanced at the door and then back at him. She was clearly unsure what to do next, so he thought he would rattle her nerves a bit to see what she could handle. "Do you mind if I ride upon your shoulder?"

"My—my shoulder?" Blythe's jawed dropped and then a look of repulsion flickered over her face before she said, "What if you ride in my pocket instead?"

"Oh." He gave the best crestfallen face he could muster and hoped it looked suitably convincing. "I have always preferred to see where I was going."

"Oh."

"How would you feel if I sat upon your head?"

"My head?" She folded her arms. "Certainly not. Prince or no, I am not allowing an amphibian to travel in my hair!"

And there was the spoiled child he knew lurked within the seventeen-year-old young woman. "Really?" He hopped forward a bit. "I am a guest."

"Yes. But—"

"One who risked his life to fetch your favorite ball."

"Risked your life! Of all the—"

"And who was forced to hop the whole way to the castle and call outside the door until the butler took pity on me because you refused to keep your part of the bargain."

"Well, I explained that it was not intentional—"

"And now, after all my troubles and being so rudely treated, I am told I must be stuffed within your pocket and jiggled and bounced around as you walk in to tea instead of being given a proper, friendly perch to sit upon."

Blythe threw her hands in the air. "Of all the inane things to agree to! I should have left my ball where it was."

He laughed. "Careful, my dear—you told your mother you would have no difficulties treating me as a guest. Do you stuff all your guests into enclosed places and rattle them about?"

"Urgh! There is no reasoning with you, is there?"

"Now that I see your true colors, it is perhaps a good thing the queen is not around."

"My true colors? That I am not willing to put up with a boorish, monstrous, smelly, slimy frog?"

He shrugged. "Just so."

"Oh, for heaven's sake! Very well."

She leaned over. "You may settle upon my

shoulder as we walk to the drawing room."

"Finally!" He hopped onto her and said rather smugly, "There! It only took a small bit of negotiation to get you to agree to be somewhat decently mannered."

"Meanwhile, in this short little episode, I have come to realize what a pushy, conceited creature you are," she replied. "My, as a prince you must have wooed all the ladies with such impeccable manners."

"Careful, my dear, you—"

"I am not your dear!" Blythe suddenly shouted. "Kindly do not call me so again."

"Hmm …" He was about to respond to her churlish remark and then thought better of it. It was always more agreeable to catch the enemy off guard. Instead, he returned to his first thought. "Be wary how you insult me, princess. I do not see many suitors beating down the doors, begging for your hand, and I think I know why."

"If you are referring to me not wishing to have you sit upon my person, it is a very natural thought for any princess to have. What guest actually prostrates themselves upon their host's head? But to push yourself and force your way into doing that which is exceedingly uncomfortable for me proves how selfish you truly are. If you were a gracious prince, you would have been happy enough indeed to travel peeking out of my pocket!" She turned and flounced through the door, almost causing him to slip off in the process.

Chapter Seven

BLYTHE GRUMBLED UNDER HER breath.
If she had to be saddled with an animal, why
did it have to be with the most pompous frog
she had ever had the displeasure of knowing?
As she came into the drawing room, she
muttered a final jab at him. "At least it is safe
to assume why you were enchanted to begin
with!"

"What do you mean?" he whispered back.

"Why, you obviously insulted some witch
with your snobbish ways and were forced into
this as punishment."

"I beg your pardon!"

"So this is the frog!" Jeremiah exclaimed

as he approached, holding his dish of food, all grins and waggling eyebrows. "You look quite happy sitting upon my sister's shoulder."

David laughed from an overstuffed chair. "Well, for a girl who is afraid of frogs and would go screaming from them, you have certainly changed your stance now. He must be quite a remarkable frog!"

"These are my older brothers," Blythe said ruefully as she walked across the room and placed Caspian upon the tea cart. Once he was situated, she turned and pointed. "That one, sitting, is Prince David and heir to the throne, and that one, standing near the door, is Prince Jeremiah.

"This is Caspian," she said as she looked at the frog. My word! What prince was this to have such manners? He had pulled a pastry off the platter and was even now gnawing on the thing right upon the cart. "Let me get a plate for you," she exclaimed as she collected one and began to fill it with tarts and scones.

"Do not forget the sandwiches," he said as he took another bite of tart.

She leaned over and whispered, "If it were up to me, I would smash you flat this instant!"

"Would you now?" he asked, his mouth full and crumbs tumbling to the cart.

"Yes!"

"Why?"

"Because!" She was going mad. Either that or she had fallen asleep at the pond and had dreamt this whole scenario. Because— well, because apparently she wished to meet a talking frog! That was it—a talking enchanted prince. Yes. Because she did not wish to marry Nolan, and therefore her subconscious was showing her how much more difficult her life would be if she did not consider him! There. She smiled. This was all a figment of her imagination. None of it was real. Sighing, she looked down at the imaginary frog.

"You still have not answered my question. Why would you smash me flat? What in the world have I done?"

He looked so real. She reached over and touched him. He *felt* so real. Her finger caressed his smooth head.

"Mmm …" He grinned and arched up, as if asking for her to continue.

He sounded real as well. Truly, this had to be the most vivid dream she had ever experienced. Suddenly she pinched him.

Caspian jumped and yelped. "What in the blazes are you doing?"

She looked up. Her brothers began to laugh and her mother did not look pleased at all.

"Do you see him?" she asked David. "Do you see the frog sitting here by me?" She pinched Caspian again.

Jeremiah guffawed. "Honestly, Blythe! Of course we see the poor thing you are physically harming."

"Blythe Genevieve Constance! You had better move away from that frog right now."

"You see him too?" Her head began to feel decidedly fuzzy.

"What is wrong with you?" her mother asked. "Of course we see him."

"It all seems so real. All of it."

"Uh, this is real." David smiled.

Blythe shook her head and groaned. "No. I am not actually in a room watching an enchanted frog eat our tea tarts."

"That is precisely what I am doing." Caspian leaned over and gobbled up a second one. "Were you going to pass on that plate in your hand?" he asked. "I am willing to eat off a plate; however, my webbed feet do not allow me to collect one myself. And whilst attempting to wound me, you do seem to have forgotten your original errand of feeding me."

"You are not real!" Blythe exclaimed. "You are not. I am dreaming this." She pointed to her family. "I am dreaming all this. You are all in my imagination right now."

Jeremiah was laughing so hard, he was bent double. "Mother! Mother," he gasped. "May I please tell our mates about this? May I, please?"

"Certainly not! Your sister will not be made into a laughingstock."

"But it is too rich!"

"'Tis true, Mother," David chimed in. "First she has this speaking frog follow her home and now she is attempting to believe he does not honestly exist when he is clearly her particular friend!"

"Enough, you two!" The queen walked up to Blythe and touched her forehead. "Are you well, child?"

Blythe pulled away. "I do not know." Already she was becoming even more fuzzy.

"Perhaps I am not as well as I could hope."

"Can you not see that I am real?" The frog unexpectedly leaped to her shoulder, causing Blythe to shriek. "See there? Had you screeched like that in a dream, it would have awakened you. So now you have proof that you are most definitely conscious."

Blythe began to feel ill. Was this all truly happening?

"Good heavens! Get off her! She is not well." Her mother sighed and pointed. "David, Jeremiah, one of you remove this frog."

"Do you not want to touch it, Mother?" Jeremiah looked smug. "Are you afraid of him?"

"You will shut your mouth and remove the thing from your sister now or I will show you what it is like to be very afraid."

Jeremiah quickly collected the frog and set him back on the tea cart. "You had better not get up there again—the women around here are not known for their rationality. You have no idea what they could do to you at any given moment."

"Believe me, you do not have to warn me

of anything. I am quite well aware. It has been an interesting day so far, to say the least."

That did it. A princess could only take so much rudeness from her guest before she snapped. She lunged for the slimy green thing.

"Blythe, stop it!" Her mother's arm flew out and halted her. "You go to bed this instant. I do not think you are all that well, child. Indeed, you are beginning to frighten me with your crazed looks and actions. Go take a rest and sleep this madness off. Perhaps you will be better in an hour or two. We will make sure Caspian is taken care of. Now go." She pushed at Blythe, who obediently turned and walked toward the door.

Perhaps she did need to rest. The strain of the day was clearly jumbling her brain. She had never felt so completely hopeless and confused before. Slowly she made her way to her room and collapsed on the bright yellow satin coverlet. There was no need to ring for Betty, her maid, to help her—not now. Not when her fuzzy mind was finally feeling warm and all things were oddly discombobulated. She yawned. Perhaps when she woke up, she would discover it was all just a dream anyhow. Grinning, she closed her eyes.

Chapter Eight

NOLAN WATCHED AS BLYTHE slowly fluttered her eyes. He had been sitting upon the pillow next to her since Jeremiah had deposited him there about an hour ago. At first he was upset with the girl and so he did a lot of glaring in silence, but then the last ten minutes or so, something had begun to change and soften within him.

The princess had begun to stir and made these sweet humming sounds, followed by a smile. He could not fathom how or why, but it made him pause and smile too. She was quite charming asleep like this, her long lashes brushing against her cheeks. Even her full lips looked much more tempting than he remembered before.

She rolled over on her side, facing him, and snuggled further into her pillow before opening her eyes. It took a moment for her gaze to settle upon Nolan, but he knew the second it did because she grimaced slightly and closed her eyes tight.

"You are still here," she moaned before cracking one eye open.

"Yes. I am afraid you are quite stuck with me."

Blythe sighed and rolled unto her back. "I know—for thirty days. Heaven help us all."

Nolan chuckled. "You are not the most pleasant princess I have ever known. Honestly, if I were to do things over, I definitely would not have wanted that thirty-day curse. Perhaps a five-day curse would have been much better."

She glanced over. "So, are you saying you designed this enchantment? As in, you were able to negotiate such a thing?"

Nolan clamped his mouth closed. How could he be such a fool?

"What are you hiding?" She turned over

on her side again. "And another thing. How long have you been sitting there while I slept?"

He shrugged. "About an hour. Your brother set me down on this pillow. How could you sleep so long in the afternoon, anyway?"

She yawned and stretched her arms above her. "Because I am a princess, of course."

"Of course. How could I have forgotten?"

"So what are you hiding?" she asked again.

He shook his head. "Nothing you need to concern yourself over."

"No?" She blinked. "And this coming from a frog that just spent an hour watching me sleep. I should not be concerned over anything about you. No, you are not disturbing at all." She sat up and nudged him off her satin cushion. "Why would my brother place you on one of my nice pillows? He should have put you upon the foot of the bed."

"Thank you." He smirked as he adjusted himself on the duvet. It would seem that the moment he began to convince himself Blythe was a good person, he was reminded again of how horrid she actually was. There was simply no way he could ask for this woman's hand. It was not worth the years of torture, knowing she was his bride.

Suddenly he remembered the letter she had tossed in the pond and was curious to see if she would reveal why she had done so.

"Do you have a suitor?" he decided to ask when all was quiet for a few minutes.

"You do not believe I have one, do you?"

He shrugged. "I may have implied such a thing, but I am interested to see what you have to say on the matter."

She smiled brightly, almost too brightly, and brought her knees to her chin. "I have one of the most wonderful men in the world as my suitor."

He was stunned and a bit warmed. "Really?"

"Yes. He is simply marvelous. Always thinking about me and sending me little bouquets of flowers and poems and the like."

What? He looked at her earnest face and wondered briefly if she had two suitors and no one had bothered to mention it to him. "Who is it? May I ask?"

She wrapped her arms tightly around her

legs, making herself look like a vulnerable little girl. "I suppose it would not matter if you knew." She took a deep breath and locked her gaze upon him. "Prince Nolan of Hollene Court."

"Truly! I hear he is a paragon among his court." He was confused. He had never sent her any little favor, but why would she tell a falsehood about him? Was this yet another unpleasant personality trait of hers that he must live through?

"Yes, he is. And a magnificent dancer as well."

How did she know he could dance? "Is there only the *one* man who is hoping to claim your hand?" Perhaps she had him mixed up with another.

She unfolded her legs and looked down. "Yes."

When she glanced his way, he attempted to catch her eye, to find what she was not revealing, but she would not allow it. Even more interested, he asked, "So tell me about him. He sounds brilliant—every woman's dream."

"He is." She smiled. "Oh, he is just

marvelous."

"If he is so perfect, why did you throw his letter in the pond?"

"I beg your pardon. How did you know I did that?"

If she was willing to lie, so was he. "I read it while I was fetching the ball." Of course, that statement was not actually false; he had read it while he was writing it.

"Oh." She sighed and brought her knees to her chest again. "Never mind; I will not attempt to paint him in a better light. You obviously know the worst now." She sighed again.

The worst? What was the girl on about? "I thought it was an exceptional letter! What was in it to create this sadness in you?"

She looked at him then. He was shocked to see her eyes shimmering with unshed tears that she quickly blinked away. "I forgot who I was speaking to. Of course you would think the letter excellent—you are a prince." Blythe reached down and twirled a bit of fabric from the duvet with her fingers. "However, perhaps I can teach you something before you make the same mistake Prince Nolan does while addressing the girl you hope to marry."

"You wish to give me advice on how to deal with a female?" He did not know whether to laugh or be appalled, but the look on her face checked him from commenting on either emotion.

"Yes."

"What did he do wrong?"

"*Does,* not *did.* He is still doing it."

As she fiddled with the fabric, he wondered what she could be speaking about. Had he not done everything in his power to confirm to her how eager he was for this courtship? Had he had not shown himself time and time again to be steadfast by proving his worth to her? What more could the girl want?

After a few moments, she whispered, "He does not see me."

There! There it was again, the same nonsense she had said at the pond. Except now he was more confused than ever. Of course he saw her! He wrote her, did he not? Why were females so difficult? He looked up and realized she was waiting for him to say something. "Oh, uh, what do you mean?" he asked.

"I was lying just now when I told you Prince Nolan is perfect.   I did not want you to know how miserable the situation actually is. I knew you would mock me even more when you knew the truth of it because honestly, if he were to come to me and ask for my hand this instant, I would reject him."

Chapter Nine

"WHAT?" NOLAN FELT HIS heart drop. "Are you certain?"

"Yes," Blythe said as she placed her chin on her knees. "He is literally the very last man I could ever want. He is the direct opposite of all those qualities I mentioned earlier. He is simply too engrossed in himself to need anyone else."

Nolan slowly let that sink in. For some reason, his heart had begun to beat uncommonly fast and he was not sure what feeling this was that coursed through him. "What do you mean? Has he done something untoward?"

"No." She closed her eyes briefly and then opened them again. "It is not that at all. We have never even met. It is simply that he does not care about me."

For the first time he noticed how deep and brown her eyes were—they were remarkably pretty. "Why would you say that?"

She grinned regretfully and sighed. "Because if he did, he would have asked about me, and he never does. Prince Nolan sends sheets and sheets of his own accomplishments, but has not once thought to ask about mine. Not any of my favorite things, my home, my thoughts—nothing. It is always only about him and his favorites. Just once, I would love to read a letter from my intended that asked me how I was doing or what I cared about most."

Those beautiful eyes began to shimmer with unshed tears again. "Caspian, I am sorry I am not what you expected a host to be. I am sorry I forgot our promise and treated you so very ill. I am not myself lately—I am worried. I am confused and concerned about a most decidedly unhappy future. All my life, I have gone ignored and been cast aside. And I have always had hopes that my future husband would be the one to see me and truly love me."

He felt his heart shatter when a small tear crept down her cheek and puddled onto her knee. Was he really that dimwitted to have treated her like this?

"I cannot have that hope now. It is simply gone." She brushed at her cheek. "When I threw that note in the pond, it was truly the last straw. I know I will never be seen by him. He will in no way care for me or consider my opinion valuable."

But it still did not explain her letters to him. Did he judge her too harshly? "And what have you written him in reply?"

"Ugh." She inhaled and sat up more fully, crossing her legs beneath her dress, and then chuckled. "Oh, the most dreadful things, actually."

Nolan watched that smile for a moment. "You were jesting in your letters to him?"

"Goodness, yes! I was mocking him." Another surprising giggle burst out as she wiped at her tears. "Thank you! I needed the laugh."

He was confused. "What do you mean?

How were you mocking him?"

"With all of his boring accomplishments he would tell me about, I decided to treat him as he treated me." She grinned. "It was quite fun to write him then, so much better than the chore it was a year ago."

"Just a moment." He shook his head. "You have been teasing Prince Nolan for a year now?" Could he be hearing her correctly?

"Yes."

The minx! "What would you say?"

She chuckled and waved her hand. "Oh, anything, really. Mostly I take the letter he sends me and then write him a female imitation of the exact thing, assuming that if he truly likes to converse only of himself, that is what he would wish me to do as well." She grinned and bit her lip. "I did have fun lamenting about the boorishness of the castle and horridly dull days at court. I became a simpering, pampered princess and hid away all of my true ideals and feelings, just allowing a very surface view of what I imagine any selfish girl would be like."

"Do you find me selfish, then?" he asked

before it dawned on him what he had said.

"You?" Blythe blinked. "No. Well, not overly so. Why would you say something like that?"

Perhaps he was better off near the pond where the foxes could find him. "I, uh, was just concerned that because you see Prince Nolan as self-centered, you might believe that was the case with all princes."

"Oh." She shrugged. "I would not know. I have only met a few at the different galas and events my mother has hosted, and then of course there are my brothers—who, while good men, are still my brothers and treat me as a sister. They are not a fair evaluation of how a prince would be, I should think."

"So I am, in essence, the first prince you have the opportunity of knowing?"

"You are definitely the first prince I have ever been this close to, with the exception of my brothers."

"Well, then." He hopped toward her. "You are in for a treat. Prince Nolan has been extremely lax in his duties toward you, but I find myself quite willing to make up for it. Since we have a month together, I will most likely drive you mad with all my questions and curiosities. I find you much more fascinating than I originally expected and am even more eager to see what will become of all this."

Her eyes searched his for a moment before she asked, "What did you have in mind?"

"I would simply like to know who you are, Princess Blythe McKenna."

"Honestly?"

"Of course."

"Do you know you are the very first person to have stated such a thing to me?"

"Am I?"

"Yes."

"Then perhaps it is a good thing I became enchanted and rescued your ball for you. Every beautiful princess deserves someone to truly see her."

Chapter Ten

IT HAD BEEN A couple of weeks since that infuriating frog had come into her life, and already Blythe began to wonder what she would ever do without him. She thought back to that first day when she had opened her eyes to find him sitting upon her bed watching her sleep. He was such a sweetheart then, but then later that evening when he insisted on using one of her pillows, she could have cheerfully strangled him.

"What do you mean, you wish to use one of my pillows?" she had asked him, astounded the forward frog would make such a request of her. It was always cold at this hour, and she in just her robe and nightclothes did not wish to be standing at her door whispering in the dead of the night with an impolite visitor.

"What? Have you perchance attempted to sleep on one of those horrid cushions you have supplied for guests? No? Well, maybe you should before someone even more important than I comes to stay the night."

"Are you saying our beds are uncomfortable?" No one had ever complained before.

"I am saying the pillows are a disgrace. I have been attempting to sleep for the past three-quarters of an hour and I cannot find a place to rest that does not have some lump or another wedging into my backside."

"And so you have made your way from the guest bedroom into my room to tell me you wish to sleep on one of my pillows?"

"No. You misunderstand me." He sighed. "I have hopped all the way to tell you I *will* be sleeping on one of your pillows."

"Good heavens!" she hissed. "You cannot just demand whatever it is you wish."

"I can and I will. Even a frog needs sleep. So go on and get me that nice satin one your brother set me down upon while I waited for you earlier today."

"Do you have any idea how much I wish I could throttle you right now?" she asked as she made her way over to the bed and collected the pillow.

He laughed. "Probably as much as I am ready to burn the pillow I was attempting to sleep upon."

Suddenly the image of Caspian dragging the thing with his mouth and tossing it into the fire caused her to smile, and she gave in as she let out a long whoosh of air. "I am sorry you cannot get to sleep. I did not have any idea the cushions were that bad." She tucked the pillow under her arm and bent over to scoop Caspian up. She placed him on her shoulder. "You are welcome to use my pillow."

"And forgive me," he said in a softer tone. "I am incredibly grouchy at night when I cannot sleep."

She chuckled as she walked out the door. "And I am incredibly cross when I have been awakened from a deep sleep." Her bare feet quickly headed down the dark corridor toward the guest wing. Why did she always forget about putting on her slippers at night?

"Good. Then we can be bad-tempered together."

Caspian settled right down on the new pillow and sighed when she placed them on the bed in the guest room. "You are an angel," he whispered as he yawned. "Thank you a thousand times over."

Blythe closed the door, but not before taking the offending cushion with her to show the queen in the morning. And then as rapidly as possible, she raced back up the corridor, tossed the old cushion onto a chair, and jumped into her thankfully still-warm bed. Snuggling into her own soft pillows, she had thought of the frog until she fell back asleep.

Blythe grinned at the memory as the maid helped her put on a pretty green gown.

Since that night two weeks ago, theirs had been a relationship full of definitely frustrated sparks, but there were also endearing moments as well. He was indeed nothing like she expected a prince to be. So thoughtful at times, so exasperating, but mostly what made her enjoy his company more than anyone she had been around was the fact he was so surprisingly humorous.

What girl did not care for someone who could make her laugh?

It was such a refreshing respite from her hours of boredom around the castle grounds and pond before he came. Her mother had never allowed much freedom for her daughters, and now that Blythe was no longer young enough to need a governess, she really had very little else to occupy herself with, except needlepoint and the like, until now.

The maid held out Blythe's short boots and she stepped into them, and then waited while they were laced up. Blythe's light-brown hair was done in a series of crisscrossed braids that formed an elegant bun. The style had taken a good quarter of an hour longer than usual that morning, but had been worth it. She felt so pretty in the green dress and with her fine hair.

"Thank you," she said as she left the maid and then walked down the corridor. She could hear giggling and a pianoforte playing in the music room and so assumed Caspian was with her sisters again. She promptly made her way there.

Smiling, she peeked into the doorway of the large room and watched Andalyn and Karielle picking out a duet on the instrument, with Caspian nodding his head in rhythm as he sat on top.

Their music teacher had not been overly fond of the disruptive frog at first, but had come to accept his interference as a part of the daily routine when it was obvious how much the girls loved him.

Actually, Caspian seemed to fit in remarkably well with all of the family. Her mother even enjoyed his political discussions after suppers in the drawing room. He knew so many facts about the surrounding kingdoms and enjoyed sharing his views and educating them on others they had been misinformed about.

All of that good coming from one small frog—how did he do it? How was he able to so easily capture the hearts of those around him? With his presence, he had managed to make her feel as though she belonged. As if she were truly a part of this family.

He was magic.

The girls started to sing and Caspian

joined in. It was a happy little ditty, but not entirely made for his voice.

Blythe giggled.

"You sound like a toad!" exclaimed ten-year-old Karielle in a fit of giggles herself.

Andalyn, never wanting to be outdone, said, "But he is one. He is supposed to sound like that."

"Thank you," Caspian said with a short bow. "Though I am not sure I would have preferred either comment, thank you nonetheless." He glanced up then and caught Blythe looking at him. "Hello there! So you have finally woken up and decided to join the rest of us, sleepyhead."

"I was not sleeping. I was waiting on my hair to be styled," she said as she came into the room.

"I see that. It looks very fetching."

She bent down at the pianoforte and he easily hopped onto her shoulder.

"Where to, fair lady?" he asked as she straightened back up and began to walk out of the room. They both ignored the protests of her sisters.

"I thought we would have a real adventure

today." She grinned.

"Oh, dear. And the past couple of weeks have not been?"

"No. Not like this." She looked around the empty hallway. "Do you notice my hair? It is done for an exact purpose. It is time you found out my secret. We are going to the village."

"Great mercy. The princess cannot simply scamper about the town of her own free will. Your mother would have palpitations if she knew of such madness. Do you realize the danger you put yourself in?"

"I know." Blythe smirked. "Which is why we shall go in disguise!"

Chapter Eleven

"WHAT ARE WE DOING here?" Nolan asked as they ducked into the third village shop within ten minutes. "Who are you looking for?" She had pulled a rather plain brown dress over her green one. It had lashings up each side which she had tied into neat bows and added flowers to her hair. Indeed, when she was done, Princess Blythe looked exactly like any village maiden. Once they got to town, she placed him in her pocket, and he immediately peeked out of it.

"It has been a couple of weeks, so I am not sure where they plan to meet me," Blythe answered. "I am making a quick sweep of all five of the stores that are our normal meeting spots."

"Such intrigue. What in the world is this secret of yours?" he whispered as she swerved to avoid a rather large man carrying a bag of flour. "What vagabonds could you possibly come here to meet? And how often do you do this?"

"Hush. You will see in a moment." She stopped and said a brief hello to one of the shoppers before rounding a corner with baskets of vegetables stacked upon a table. "Now be quiet. How will I explain a talking frog to the villagers? You will soon understand all."

"Very well," he grumbled while his mind tried to sort through what mischief the girl had gotten herself into. Many of the villagers appeared to know her as one of their own. No one seemed to bat an eyelash at the girl. But what was she doing?

"Goodness," she mumbled as she made her way into a clothing shop. "There they are. I was beginning to get worried."

Caspian looked beyond the ready-made dresses for sale and a few shirts and trousers for men. As she continued to walk toward the back of the room, he finally saw who she was speaking about. Children!

There were about eight grubby-looking boys and girls all huddled in the back of the store near the boots. They remained as noiseless as possible as she approached.

"Hello there," she mouthed and then put her finger to her lips.

The children all smiled in return. One adorable little girl in braids was missing her two front teeth.

What was the princess thinking, meeting with such children?

Blythe turned without a sound and began to walk out of the building. She paused a moment at the door and then beckoned the lot to follow her on a pathway where they headed beyond the village altogether. The little row of children slipped around thick underbrush and down a hidden trail right into the forest. They walked silently for about five minutes until they came to a beautiful clearing and then finally the princess turned and smiled.

"Well, we made it!"

"Yay!" the group cheered as they rushed

forward and sat several feet away. They had obviously done this many times—it was as if they had special places in the grassy meadow.

"Now will you tell me what is going on?" Nolan asked.

"I think I will show you to the children," she said, clearly ignoring his question. "I bet they would love to meet a talking frog." She began to pull him from her pocket.

"Halt!" he commanded sternly. "Unless you inform me of what mischief this is and why all the secrecy, I will not speak one word to those children and you will look a fool."

She sighed. "Can you not go along and figure it out for yourself?"

"Certainly not." He had to remain firm to protect them both. "Blythe, if you are breaking some law with these boys and girls, I will have no part in it."

She giggled and then glanced toward the patient children sitting in a semicircle about thirty feet away. "Just a moment," she called to them. "I have a surprise for you." Turning her back to the group, she pulled him out and held him in front of her. "Very well."

He looked into those brown eyes—the

intensity in them shook his core. He realized she was about to tell him something she had never told anyone before. "What is it?"

She shook her head and then smiled ruefully. "It is not something grand or even wonderful. The school mistress died a few years back. My father had orchestrated the schooling to begin with against the wishes of his queen. The teacher passed about a year after my father, and my mother, who had always disagreed with the education of lower-class citizens, just simply never hired on another school mistress. It was still another year or so before I knew of the issue. After overhearing the maids gossiping, I have been fulfilling the role of teacher for the past eighteen months."

"Indeed!" It felt as if his heart were expanding. "You honestly care for these children? Mere villagers?"

"Of course! How could I not?"

He would never have thought of his own subjects like this, not nearly enough to devote a year and a half to the cause of their education. Great heavens! "So why the secrecy?"

"The guards!" She looked shocked, as if he should have been able to figure it out on his own. "If they knew what I was doing, my mother would put a stop to it all."

"I cannot imagine your mother being that heartless."

Blythe smirked. "She is a good woman. She is a brilliant mother and ruler, but she does still maintain a few of those backward ideals that I do not." She turned and looked at the little group awaiting her. "As you can see, I only have a few who are willing to risk coming and learning. If I could have my way, I would be teaching them all openly in the town."

"How often do you come? And why have you not brought me here before?"

"I usually do this twice a week on Tuesdays and Thursdays for a few hours. But I left word with a trusted servant that I would not be coming as usual, as I had a special house guest with me."

"So why now?"

She looked at him for a moment and then said, "Because I trust you to keep my secret. Because it is time someone knew. And because I needed to. I needed to show you what no one else has bothered to discern."

"Are you really left by yourself in that castle?"

"Yes. If I am not here, I am at the pond." She looked away. "It is easier to leave someplace and be by yourself than to be in a home full of people and know that you are alone."

Nolan looked at her pretty profile for a moment and then said, "Princess Blythe, forgive me for every false idea I had about you. You are quite different from the girl I believed you were."

She glanced back. "I am?"

"You are greater than I could have ever imagined. And I am humbled and honored that you decided to share this with me. Thank you."

"You are welcome." She blushed, and then as if she did not know how to take his compliments, simply grinned and waggled her brows, clearly hoping to change the subject. "So, now that you know all, are we ready to have some fun?"

Chapter Twelve

THEY SPENT NEARLY THREE hours laughing with the village children. Even though they were at school, so to speak, Nolan loved how Blythe created an environment for them that was much more fun than work, with songs and rhyming and games. It really felt like they were playing, and the children responded so well to it. Now if only she had been his tutor when he was a lad—he might have actually paid attention and learned more!

When Blythe had originally approached the children with Nolan sitting on her palms, one of the older girls squealed and pulled back. But the boys and the two younger girls were eager to meet him and rushed forward. Nolan and Blythe had decided she would not tell them he could speak and let it come as a surprise after several minutes.

"Do not be afraid." Blythe beckoned to the older girl. "Caspian is a good friend of mine and nothing to be frightened over."

"Can I touch him?" asked the adorable toothless child, the red bows on her braids twitching in her excitement.

"Of course you can, Charity." Blythe smiled and brought him closer. "Here. He really loves it when his head is rubbed."

She grinned and reached out a small finger, softly running it along the top of him.

He had never seen anything cuter in his life. He could not help it; he had to ruin the surprise already. "Ahh …" he said. "That feels marvelous."

She squeaked and the whole group jumped back. "He can talk?" she asked.

"I would hope so!" Nolan pretended to be affronted. "It would be incredibly dreadful if I could not."

Charity's eyes were wide. "But how can you?"

He puffed up his chest and said, "Because I am a magic frog."

Charity giggled and stepped forward again. "Ooh, I like magical things! Will you do something for us?"

The children tittered and pressed closer. He even noticed the older girl approaching the group cautiously. "I will do something none of you have ever seen before!" he said loudly in a very mysterious voice.

"What?" Charity whispered. "What will you do?"

He turned and looked up at Blythe. "Will you kneel down so I may be closer to the ground?"

She grinned and did as he asked, though he could tell she was just as curious as the children. Once he was close enough, he hopped to the end of her fingers. "Are you ready to see something that will completely amaze you?" he asked the group. He had done this particular thing plenty of times as a human whilst standing on the ground. Hopefully, with the added height of her hands and his strong frog legs, he would be able to pull the trick off easily.

"Go on, then!" called one of the boys.

"Ahem." He took a couple of steps in place and then sprang off her hands, flipping once and then landing quite deftly upon the soft grass. That was even better than he had imagined! With those legs, he could probably do two flips.

"Whoa!" the group exclaimed as they began to chatter and clap.

He looked behind him to see Blythe applauding with them.

"What did I tell you?" Nolan hopped backwards, closer to her, as he spoke to the children. "You have never seen a talking, flipping frog in your life, now have you?"

"Do it again!" one of the boys shouted.

"Yes! Again! Again!" the children chorused.

"I do not think you have much of a choice." Blythe giggled.

"Very well." He hopped into Blythe's waiting hands and said, "Raise me up about another five inches. There. That is perfect." He bounced twice and to the gasps of the children, flipped two times through the air and landed gracefully upon his webbed feet.

They cheered and another cry came out, "Once more! Please, again! Do it again!"

He thought about it for a moment, but if these children were half as rambunctious and eager as his friends had been growing up, he knew they would demand flips the whole day. "I had better not. We are here to do schooling, not watch me perform." The children groaned. "But if you do really well, I promise to show you again once we are all through."

"Wonderful!" Blythe exclaimed as she picked him up. "Come on, everyone—find your seats and we shall begin so we can watch the amazing Caspian again." As they ran ahead, she whispered, "That was simply incredible. Thank you for being kind to them."

"My pleasure." He looked right into those dark eyes. She truly was one of the most beautiful girls he had ever known. And now, it would seem, her beauty inside surpassed that of her outer appearance.

"I was afraid to tell you what I was doing when I came to the village." She glanced toward the children and then back at him. "For fear you would mock me, or not see the value of such an endeavor."

He shook his head and said seriously, "Never. I might not have thought of villagers needing instruction or learning such as this, but that does not mean that I cannot learn myself. In these few minutes, you have taught me more about how to be a good ruler than any person has. Thank you for trusting me and sharing this."

She smiled. "I have half a mind to kiss your sweet cheek; you have made me so happy!" She leaned forward.

"No!" Nolan panicked and nearly fell out of her hands when he attempted to hop away from her. "Do not kiss me!"

"Oh." Blythe flushed as she clutched him tighter so he would not fall. "I am sorry. Forgive me."

"No." His heart was racing so fast, he could not think properly. "No, you do not understand. There is nothing to forgive. You cannot kiss me. Not yet. We are not ready to face such things."

"Oh." Her voice was a bit high-pitched. "Very well, I will not think of such an idea." Clearly she was embarrassed.

He could not bear to have her believe he did not like her. "Blythe, it is the way to release the spell early. If you were to kiss me right now, I would turn into a prince. And not only do I feel like it is not the time to do so, for our sakes, we must think of the children as well. What would they do if I transformed before them?"

"My goodness!" She gasped. "Caspian, you are quite right. I am not ready to find out who you are. I have so much to sort out within myself first before I begin to think of you like that."

"Besides," he spoke softer. "If I was a prince, I would have to go home, and I am not ready to leave yet. Do you mind if we give this just a bit longer?"

She let out a relieved chuckle. "Yes! Yes, please. Let us stay just like this a little while longer. I am not ready to lose you either."

It was settled then. His heart warmed at the glow he saw within her gaze. They were beginning to understand each other. This truly was the perfect disguise—he was grateful he had done it now. However, he must find a way to ease her into accepting the fact that he was her intended before the spell was broken, or who knew how well she would understand why he had been pretending not to know her all along.

Besides, now that he knew she had been pretending because of his ill manners, he had to work through his own presumptions of her. He had to realize that all he despised about her was truly his own making. Prince Nolan was, indeed, the pompous monster she had always believed him to be. Yet, after today, he knew without a doubt that she was not nor would ever be the spoiled princess he thought.

No, she could not kiss him. There was no way he was ready to reveal himself at the moment, for how could he? To do so now would only expose the fact that he was the man she detested. The man he was beginning to detest as well.

Chapter Thirteen

AS THEY HEADED BACK to the village, Nolan wrestled within himself on how to reveal who he was. He hoped to be able to ease it in slowly without startling her, but quite frankly could not think of the best way to go about it.

Blythe stopped to purchase a few things for them to munch on at the farmers' market and then continued uphill to the castle after a quick luncheon.

Once they were far enough away from the bustling town, she pulled him out of her swaying skirts and set him on her shoulder so he could see better.

"Do you always make this long trek on foot?" he asked when they were about halfway. He could not imagine either of his sisters walking this far of their own free will.

She gave a little shrug. "Yes. I prefer to walk—I find it invigorating. Besides, though I have horses at my disposal, they would be recognized as castle property immediately. I would be much more noticeable on a horse than a girl on foot."

"You do seem to blend in remarkably well."

"I do." Her voice had a questioning tone to it, almost as if she could not believe how she managed it. "Sometimes I wonder if the villagers know who I am and are grateful, allowing me to continue in peace. And then other times I wonder if it is because they have grown so used to seeing me that they do not question my appearance anymore. I am just a regular part of the community. Whichever it is, I am grateful for the anonymity," she said as she continued forward.

He felt the briskness in her step and remembered the contented smiles upon her face throughout the day. "You really do love this, do you not?"

She took a deep breath. "I do. I do
so very much. I needed a means to feel
appreciated. I needed something to break me
free from the confines of life and learn to live.
Helping people like this is a passion I never
knew I had. And to fall so in love with serving
these brave children, it is truly the most
rewarding experience I have ever known."

He had so many comments to make to
such a speech, but what fumbled its way to
the top of the list of questions and replies was
simply, "You will become a magnificent queen
one day."

Blythe's foot caught upon something as
she stumbled a bit. "I beg your pardon?" she
said as she began to walk again.

Why did she seem so amazed? "You do
not believe me? After being in such close
proximity to you for as many days as I have
been, and now being involved in one of the
most enlightening experiences, it is quite
simply an easy assessment to make. You will
be a grand ruler indeed."

All at once, she halted. He looked up to
see her purse her lips and turn her head away.

"Blythe, what is it? Have I said something to wound you?"

She raised her head and looked at the looming castle before them, and then twisted to see the village below. Still she would not say a word.

His heart began to beat hollowly at her curious behavior. "What is wrong?"

Her voice cracked. "I—I am sorry."

Not knowing what to say, he waited for her to continue.

After a few moments, she explained, "I am overcome right now. It is nothing." She waved her hand. "Truly, nothing you have done wrong. Rather, it is hearing words I never imagined I would hear that has caused such emotions to spring forth."

"You did not believe you would be a good queen?"

"No." She turned more fully and looked out over the rooftops below them. "I did not know it was an aspiration to achieve. I just knew it as my life, my reality, that I would more than likely be queen to some kingdom somewhere."

"Hollene?" he asked, naming his own

kingdom.

"Yes, if I decided to accept Prince Nolan's proposals, though that possibility is becoming less and less every day. I do not have a mind to accept him at all now."

"It is?" Nolan's stomach clenched and suddenly he felt ill. "Why?"

She threw her arms out. "How could I marry such a man now?"

"Are you sure he is truly that vile?"

"No." She shook her head. "I am not sure. However, with each day that passes, I am convinced more wholly that is the direct opposite of anything I would be comfortable with."

"How long have these thoughts been plaguing you?"

She chuckled. "Did I not make myself clear weeks ago? For at least a couple of years now."

"So why did you not call it off before then, if you have felt so strongly?" He was genuinely curious.

"Because—because I had hope."

"And you do not now?"

"No. I do not need it anymore. Now I

have you."

The full force of her words had not sunk in before she became a flurry of emotion again.

"Let us continue on home or I will say things I may regret later," she said as she tittered nervously. "My goodness, I might have already revealed too much."

He remained quiet. It was clear by her actions that she was greatly relieved when he did not speak as they made their way up the path to the castle, but silence did not stop his mind from racing even more. Had she nearly revealed that she was in love with him? Could that possibly be where her thoughts had been? Or was he reading too much into the situation? One thing was for certain—he had never felt more misery than when she announced she would not marry Prince Nolan, so he must be developing feelings for her beyond what he could have ever imagined. For why else would his heart race so happily now if it were not the case?

Could she have actually fallen for him in this silly frog shape?

Was she really that incredible of a

woman?

All these thoughts and more continued to churn in a great tumultuous whirlwind in his mind, causing him some moments of astonished excitement and even more confusion than clarity.

He continued to ponder it as they crept into the castle. Nolan had Blythe set him down near the nursery so he could torment her sisters a bit before tea while she went in to freshen up and change in time to pour for her mother. At half past three there was not much time to tease the girls, as tea was always served at precisely four o'clock. However, one should never underestimate a frog.

He hopped into the room to the delighted squeals of the girls and then promptly disrupted the lessons on writing to focus on his flipping skills. The governess, however, was quick to adapt her lesson to include arithmetic and the amount of force it took for him to spring off the desk with the number of rotations he could make before landing upon the floor. She spent the rest of the time teaching the girls the mathematical difference between the two, using him as an example.

Andalyn was giggling when the maid peeked her head in and announced tea. "That was the most fun we have ever had learning a subject."

Karielle quickly scooped him up in her arms. "We must show Mother what we have been taught today. Do you mind doing it again?"

With those amazing back legs, he could probably jump eighty times in a row and not get tired. "I would love to, if you think she would not mind."

"Mother, mind?" Andalyn grinned. "She loves you! She would more than likely allow you to do anything and be happy about it."

"Then by all means, let us show her your new arithmetic skills," he said.

"And your splendid flipping skills!" Karielle held him close while the girls rushed down the stairs.

Chapter Fourteen

LATER THAT EVENING AFTER supper,
Blythe stepped away from the little group
in the drawing room. Caspian was now
entertaining her brothers with his flipping
tricks. The poor guy—he had been jumping
and spinning all day. He had to be tired,
though from the excited banter behind her, he
definitely did not seem to mind much.

She smiled as she opened the balcony
doors and stepped out into the moonlight. The
soft summer breeze caressed her arms as she
walked out toward the edge and set her lantern
upon the balustrade. This was quiet and
peaceful.

Leaning over the barrier, she looked down to the stream in the valley below the castle. Her great-grandfather had chosen this particular mountain to build his castle upon. The balcony views never failed to impress her. It was so beautiful out here, especially with gentle wind dancing about her. She looked across the valley and mountain directly in front of her. It was such a pretty place, an ideal view for quiet reflection and pondering on oneself.

She sighed and sat upon the balustrade, the blue skirts of her evening gown spreading around her. There was so much about Caspian she longed to find out. So many more questions she wanted to ask him. It was such a surprise that she trusted him enough to share her secret of teaching the children.

If he were really to turn into a prince again in just a couple more weeks, he could very well be someone she could love. No matter how handsome or how plain a prince he was, that did not matter. Her mind flitted over the thought of Prince Nolan, but she quickly dismissed him. She could never feel comfortable around someone of his arrogance and selfishness. She needed more out of life than pretending to be a snobbish girl for him. She needed substance and understanding from a relationship.

Nolan seemed so unstable. She had been forgotten for too long to ever feel settled with a man with his characteristics. And her mother, her brothers, her sisters—her whole family loved Caspian.

Was it wrong of her to imagine a man such as he in her life always?

"What has you so quiet out here?" asked Caspian as he hopped toward her.

"Hello." She grinned. "I was just enjoying a moment."

"Would you mind if I joined you?"

Suddenly her heart twisted, and she felt near to tears. There was no reason for such silliness, but it was how she felt all the same. "Yes. Yes, I would love company."

"And why does your voice take on such a tone? Are you well?"

She chuckled and shook her head. "I do not know what is wrong with me, why the unexpected emotions."

He hopped onto the banister next to her

and peered up at her face. "Princess Blythe?"

Just seeing him next to her, so calm and steady and caring—he genuinely cared for her—the tears began to blur her vision.

"Blythe, what is it?"

And then she understood, as odd and as sad as it was. She knew why it was so easy to fall in love with him. "Forgive me." She dashed at her tears. "It is nothing. Just the surprise of being noticed, I believe."

"What do you mean?"

She took a shaky breath. What *did* she mean? "You came. You looked for me. You found me." She glanced back at the door that was ajar. "I step away from my family and come here, usually tossing my ball, many a warm night to reflect on life only to return to find the room empty and dark."

"No one has sought you out before?"

She wiped at her eyes again. "No one has ever joined me on the balcony."

"Until now."

Her eyes met his green gaze. "Until now."

His face took on such an image of sadness and pity for brief moment that she blinked and looked back out toward the valley below them.

"Thank you," she whispered.

"I do not know about you, but, uh, this prince prefers the company of an enchanting princess much more than he does her siblings and mother. I would always find you. You are the reason I am here."

She glanced back at him, her heart beating strangely within her chest. "Truly?"

"Yes."

"Caspian, what are we to do when you transform back into a prince? What happens then?"

"Well, I suppose I go back to my old life."

"And were you happy in that life?" she asked, eager for his answer.

"Of course. I enjoyed myself very much."

"Oh." If he was so content, how could she wish him to change that for her?

He hopped a step toward her until he was right next to the lantern. "What exactly are you asking? You seem troubled."

"I am, I think." She stood up and leaned against the edge. "My family is so keen on me marrying Prince Nolan and I just cannot do so. I clearly cannot. I fear even the sight of him will induce me to become ill."

"Well, I am sorry to hear you say that."

She looked at him. "You are?"

"More than you will ever know."

Did he wish her to marry Nolan then, and not think of himself as a suitor? Did he feel as if he had intervened somehow? She tried again. "Caspian, it does not matter. I will never marry him. I did not wish it to begin with, and I simply cannot. I prefer a man so much greater than he is."

"I see." He hopped from the banister onto the ground. "Come and let us go inside now. I wish to spend these last days with you perfectly. It is not time to think of the future—it is time to enjoy the present. Besides, I have a mind to beat you soundly at chess."

"Chess? Are you mad?" She chuckled and walked a step toward him. "You do not even have hands."

"'Tis true. I will have to depend upon your mercy to move my pieces for me. But since I am quite the champion at home, I fear your only defense will be to cheat and move them in the exact place I would not wish them to be."

Blythe gasped. "What? Me, cheat? I

would never!" She put her hands on her
hips. "Very well then, Mr. Frog Prince, I shall
accept your challenge. I am in no way a good
player at chess, but your ego has brought out
the champion in me. I can tell already I shall
beat you soundly in record time—without
cheating!"

"Oh, ho!" He laughed. "Well, then, my
fair princess, lead the way! I am all eagerness
to see such a woman best me."

Blythe had never had more fun losing
such a silly game in her life. He was honestly
the most humorous companion she had ever
had. Their game soon became a nightly
ritual—full of laughter and howling and mad
bantering skills.

And she lost every single match.

They were still teasing one another about
chess as they walked back from the village a
week or so later. Blythe had a splendid day
teaching again, but was now enjoying the
sparring Caspian was quick to induce.

"You are so awful at chess that my blind,
lame grandmother could soundly whip you!"
he taunted.

"Me? Me?" She giggled, knowing full

well he had no such grandmother. "And what of your ego, sir? That head is so large, I fear another win of yours and it may explode and a whole clump of green mess will land upon the game and me."

He pretended to gulp. "I believe you would like to see such a thing happen!"

She was just about to reply when they rounded the back corner of the flower garden and walked into the castle stable yard.

They both gasped in unison.

There sat a beautiful white coach and four with the royal Hollene family crest painted in bright green and gold on the side.

Prince Nolan! What in the world was he doing here?

Chapter Fifteen

BLYTHE'S STOMACH DROPPED AND her hands began to shake as she stepped into the side entrance of the castle. Why would Prince Nolan show up now, of all times? She was not certain she was ready to meet him. Not yet. Not when things were beginning to make sense with Caspian. Ugh. If her mother were to take a fancy to Nolan, there would be no stopping the wedding ceremony.

And then she would have to leave the castle, for there would definitely not be a bride in attendance during the reading of the nuptials.

What did Prince Nolan want?

Goodness! Perhaps he was worried about why she had not written him back. She had forgotten to after tossing his letter into the pond. Well, how was she to remember something like that? Especially with the arrival of Caspian—everything else seemed to have been forgotten. For the last couple of weeks, all she had thought about was the frog.

"If you drop me off here," Caspian said, "I will distract your mother and the guest until you can change out of your village attire."

"Yes, Mother will no doubt want me in attendance immediately." Blythe set the frog near the arched entry of the grand corridor. The drawing room was just down along the way from where they were. Already she could hear her mother's laughter coming from within it. "Let her know I am freshening up before I make my appearance," she said as she watched him hop down the hall.

As swiftly as possible, she made her way up the servants' stairs and into her room. Her maid met her there and helped remove the brown frock and stash it in the bottom of the chest beneath the extra blankets at the foot of her bed. It was where they had first decided to hide the plain dress in case the queen ever went through her wardrobe. It was this particular maid who had first told Blythe of the children's lack of a schoolteacher, and together they formed this plan.

Blythe removed the flowers from her hair and the maid was quick to replace them with pretty gold ribbons. They brushed at her green gown as Blythe stood at the looking glass and turned from side to side to see if any of the day's dirt could be found upon it. Once she was deemed presentable enough, she thanked the maid and nervously walked down to the drawing room.

She took a deep breath just before the footman opened the door.

There, perched charmingly upon the high-backed chair, was a plump woman in rows of lavender ruffles. Her mother sat on the adjoining seat, with her back to the door, and Caspian was on top of the settee.

Her mother turned at the woman's smile in Blythe's direction. "Blythe, you are here at last!" she said in a gently scolding tone. "My goodness, I sent for you nearly three-quarters of an hour ago."

Blythe curtsied. "I beg your pardon. Caspian and I were outdoors."

Her mother waved her hand. "Yes, yes. No doubt down at your pond. Now come here—I would like to introduce you to Queen Bethany of Hollene Court, Prince Nolan's dear mother and one of my most particular friends from our school days."

"How do you do?" Blythe walked across the room and deeply curtsied before Queen Bethany.

"My! You are quite lovely!" she said as she crooked her finger to gesture Blythe in closer. "If I am not mistaken, you look exactly like your grandmama, Queen Mary Elizabeth I."

"Aye, she does. My mother was an exceptional beauty," stated Mary. "At supper, you shall meet my two elder sons and my two younger daughters as well. Then you may gauge who is the most like whom." Her mother grinned and waved Blythe toward the settee. "Sit next to your companion, dear. Bethany and I were just laughing at some of the amusing things Caspian has said to keep us entertained while we waited for you." Another soft ring of annoyance came through her tone of voice at the last few words.

"I hope he did not frighten you," Blythe said to Queen Bethany. "We are so used to him now, I did not even think how you must have felt when you saw him hop in."

"He is fine, dear. And quite a charming rascal as well." She grinned at the frog, and Blythe was surprised to see her slip in a sly wink.

Mary laughed. "Oh, do not let Bethany fool you! She jumped as high as anyone I have seen when he first came in and said hello."

"'Tis only because I was not prepared to see him like that."

"Do you mean, to see a talking frog? Or just to see a frog in general going about the place?" Blythe asked.

"No, I meant to see *him* like *that*."

"Well, you have yet to tell us why you came, Queen Bethany," Caspian declared, a bit overly loud. "And I am sure it does not have anything to do with secrets of Prince Nolan's that you should be keeping, does it?"

Blythe glanced at him. Why was he

behaving so oddly? "Are you implying that she is keeping something from us?"

Mary laughed before Bethany or Caspian could reply. "What heaviness is in this room! I will not have it. We are a merry party who are together now and that is all that matters."

"'Tis true," Caspian said. "Forgive my rudeness, Queen Bethany."

"No matter," she said. "I have simply come to see for myself what Princess Blythe is like. I have heard so many things about you from my son, my dear." She grinned. "And I decided it was about time to come meet you personally. I find it is the best way to truly get to know someone—face-to-face like this. Do you not agree?"

"I do." Blythe chuckled, liking her already. "Though I cannot imagine what Prince Nolan has relayed about me."

"Yes, but I am sure you would not be interested in hearing any of it," Caspian said.

"No, on the contrary. I am very curious to see how my betrothed speaks of me to others. I feel any woman would be. It is only natural." She looked at Queen Bethany.

"Would you mind sharing what has intrigued you so that you have come out to meet me?"

Chapter Sixteen

NOLAN GULPED. HIS MOTHER would
not really be that brainless as to actually tell
Blythe what he had thought of her, would she?

She glanced at him and gave him another
wink. Good grief. She really was that
dim. Of course she would tell everything.
Somehow, someway, she probably believed
it would help him. He opened his mouth to
intervene and stop the inevitable, but she was
much quicker.

"Oh, you know how young men talk to
their mothers. You are never fully clear on
what they are truly thinking. He will say one
thing today and then tomorrow tell me the

direct opposite."

Nolan breathed a sigh of relief. It would seem he was safe after all.

"I can agree with you there!" Mary laughed. "My boys will forever tell me one thing and I will believe it is truly their opinion on the matter. Yet, when I relay such things to someone else, it is all they can do to contradict me at every turn, specifically clarifying that they had never meant their original opinion after all."

"Are you saying he has changed his mind about me?" Blythe asked, her features scrunched in confusion.

"Oh, goodness, no!" Bethany leaned forward. "No, his opinion of you has always been the same. If anything, it may have become more fervent throughout the last few months or so, but he has always portrayed the same interest in the arrangement as ever before."

"Well, that is fine then," Mary exclaimed with a look at her daughter. "It is nice to know there is a steadfast man in your home."

"Steadfast?" Blythe shook her head. "But moments ago, you implied he was not firm.

Have I perchance missed something?"

"Oh! I did, did I not?" All at once his mother began to giggle nervously. "So it would seem I have. Well, then!" Her giggle continued and rose several notches.

Nolan closed his eyes. This did not bode well for his future happiness.

"Is there something you wish to say to me?" Blythe asked as Bethany continued to laugh.

Nolan could not imagine what Blythe must think of his mother, for truly she was behaving as a woman caught in a lie.

The look his mother gave him clearly begged for support of some kind. At least she was wise enough not to wish extra trouble upon him. He sighed. How was he supposed to get her out of this mess? One thing was for certain—he needed to make sure she realized that his opinion had changed. "Well, I for one wish Prince Nolan was here with you now. Then everyone would know the truth of his feelings and we would not be in such confusion," he said.

Bethany laughed louder and then said, "Oh! Goodness. I was not sure what to say—

but you have helped me so very much! Thank you, Caspian." She sighed and wiped at her eyes. Apparently she had been so nervously laughing, tears had formed.

But it would seem she had received his silent message to let him speak for himself. Nolan released his own breath of relief just as she continued to talk.

"However, since my son is not here, I feel it is my duty to relay the following ..." She looked directly at Blythe. "He has frankly not been impressed with your letters and feels you are the last person he would ever wish to marry."

Blythe and her mother both gasped.

Nolan groaned. Oh, my word! This was worse than he could have imagined.

"I beg your pardon?" Mary exclaimed. "My daughter is a fine example of an exemplary princess. It would take a complete moronic beast not to see the wonderful qualities she possesses! It is your son I worry about."

"Mother!" Blythe looked upset. "Please do not. It is fine."

"Well, I was only relaying what he has

said to me," Bethany said with a huff. "It is why I came, to see for myself if she truly was the spoiled child he believed her to be."

"Spoiled?" Mary stood up. "My Blythe spoiled?"

"Wait!" Blythe called out from the settee.

Bethany quickly stood up too. "And willful and arrogant."

Mary took a step forward, her face redder than Nolan thought possible upon a human being. "Take it back!" she snapped. "Your son must be the epitome of the most uncouth louse who was ever born!"

"Nolan?" Bethany inhaled sharply and pointed her finger at the other queen. "I will have you know there is not a greater man in all the surrounding kingdoms than my son, nor is there a better judge of character!"

"Wait!" Blythe said again as she stood up.

Mary took another step forward. "Your son would not know how to judge a pig's backside from a superior stallion's rump!"

"Take it back!" Bethany raged. "You have no right!"

"And you have no right to say such things of my daughter!"

"I have every single right, if it pertains to the happiness of my son. Those are his feelings on the matter and therefore what is the truth. If you did not wish to hear the truth, I suggest you raise your daughter to become a bit more pleasing to the rest of the world!"

"Do not say such things about her!" Caspian shouted.

"Wait! Halt!" Blythe stepped in between the two livid women. "Enough!"

Caspian tried again. "You do not know—"

Mary interrupted. "Blythe, move out of the way. Bethany and I have much more to discuss."

"No, you do not!" Blythe put her hands on her hips.

Bethany's jaw dropped. "Well, I never! To see such rudeness and blatant disrespect in a princess! It would definitely seem my son was wholly correct in his assumption of you."

"No," Caspian called, but Bethany glared.

"Please!" Blythe put her hand up to stop her mother from retaliating and turned to Queen Bethany. "It is perfectly all right. I do not wish to marry Prince Nolan, and I am grateful that he does not harbor such ideas about me. Indeed, I truly believe we would be much better suited if we were each to marry someone else entirely."

"Very well!" Bethany exclaimed, smirking. "I can see that perhaps we were hasty in this betrothal. Your promise can definitely become dissolved. What do you say, Mary?"

"I find that completely satisfactory. As of right now, Prince Nolan and Princess Blythe will never wed!"

"Perfect!" Blythe genuinely smiled, her eyes sparkling. "For he is truly the last man I would ever wish upon myself."

Nolan's heart dropped.

She would never like him now.

And all of this was for naught.

Everyone seemed to be celebrating the fact that the two of them would never wed.

If only they had thought to ask him.

He watched the women make up and apologize to each other in stiff politeness. With a final glance at Blythe's happy face, he hopped off the settee and slowly made his way out of the room and down the long corridor.

Perhaps it would be best if he just headed home. There was a coach waiting for him, which would provide a much quicker way home. Besides, now that everyone else was so cheerful, perhaps he could find a way to become joyful too.

Chapter Seventeen

BLYTHE SMILED AND GLANCED toward Caspian. He was not there. Where did he go? She looked around the room—the floor, chairs, tables, everywhere. He was most definitely not there.

It was not like Caspian to leave without mentioning where he was going first. She shrugged. Perhaps he would be back shortly.

As her mother rang for tea, Blythe sat on the settee, knowing she would be expected to pour for the queens. She was also very well aware that the frog would not miss the opportunity for tea and would come hopping back into the room very soon. Then she would be sure to quiz him on where he had been.

"Where is the frog?" Bethany asked when she looked up and noticed he was missing.

Mary glanced up as well. "Is Caspian not with us?"

"No, I think he went out for a few minutes. I am sure he will be back shortly," Blythe said.

"He is more than likely playing with the girls upstairs," Mary said.

"Probably. He will return soon."

However, when tea came, there was still no Caspian.

In fact, after an hour of boring, tension-filled polite talk, since the two queens were desperately attempting to appease the other after their horrendous start that afternoon, Blythe finally excused herself.

She made her way up to the nursery where her sisters were doing their studies. Peeking inside the door, she saw that they were both reading quietly while the governess searched through papers. There was no sign of Caspian anywhere. After a few seconds, she caught Karielle's attention and beckoned her to come.

"Have you seen Caspian?" she asked

quietly.

"No. Not since this morning at the pianoforte. Why?"

"I was just curious. I have not seen him for a little while, so wondered if he came up here with you two."

"No."

The governess looked up and Blythe whispered, "Very well, thank you. Perhaps he is taking a nap."

Shutting the door, she quickly made her way to his room and was surprised to see that it looked tidier than usual. Her pillow was tucked nicely against the wall and everything looked to be in order. The room also felt eerily empty, as if he were actually gone and not just hiding away somewhere.

Her heart began to beat faster and she took a deep breath as she reminded herself to remain calm. This meant nothing. He could be anywhere. She was just allowing her imagination to get the better of her.

After checking her room to see if he was there, and then the music room, Blythe decided her best course of action was to run down to the pond and see if he opted for a swim or something. He was indeed a frog, after all, and more than likely needed a nice cool soak. He had come often to the pond with her over the last couple of weeks as they talked and babbled about life. He would swim while she tossed her ball.

As she headed there, she kept an eye on the ground to see if she could find him. There were so many bushes and dips and dangers along this path. Any sort of threat could have lurked and snatched him up, like a hawk or woodland animal. She took a deep breath. Worrying was not going to do anything but make her worry more.

With her stomach in knots, she approached her favorite rock and leaned over the pond. It was still and sparkling and completely empty.

"Caspian?" she called. "Caspian? Are you here?"

She was not going to panic. She was not going to panic.

Her hands began to shake as she sat down upon the boulder.

What had happened? Did she do something to frighten him away? Did he not wish to be with her anymore?

She knew these were irrational thoughts—he was most likely somewhere very rational and fine—but she could not help thinking of him.

He was gone.

She buried her face in her hands and began to cry.

If she were perfectly honest with herself, she would see he was truly her best friend. The only creature who knew her secrets, and who she loved with all her heart.

Blythe gasped and wiped at a few tears.

She loved him. He was annoying and demanding at times, but so sweet and dear and funny and wonderful. He was just wonderful.

Her Caspian. He could not leave her now.

He could not! Soon he would change back into a prince, and she had no idea who that was. She gasped again. She would never be able to find him! Oh, no!

She groaned and kicked at a pebble near her foot. She should have kissed him that day when she had the chance! Never mind that she did not think she was ready. She was ready. She was more than ready. She needed him.

"Caspian? Caspian?" She stood and called. "My frog prince! Come back. Please, tell me where you are."

Plopping back down upon the rock, she said, "I need you. I cannot return to a life where I am forgotten. Please, please do not go."

She could not accept this. She could not! There were still many other places he could be. The castle was huge! He could be trapped somewhere and needed her. She would not sit and become a watering pot now, not when the prince she loved was missing.

She rushed back to the palace and arrived just as the Hollene coach was leaving.

Queen Bethany halted the carriage and had the coachman draw up near Blythe. "Goodbye, my dear," Bethany said. "I hope I did not offend you with my son's thoughts earlier."

"No. Not at all." Blythe curtsied. "I wish you safe travels."

"Why, thank you." She smiled and then asked suddenly, "May I ask something?"

"You may."

"Tell me honestly. How did you become friends with the frog? How can you do it?

Does he not repulse you?"

"Caspian?" Blythe was shocked. "Of course not! Why, he is the dearest, most wonderful person I have ever known."

"Person? You think of him as a human?"

"I simply cannot think of him in any other light. He is as dear to me—no, more so—than any man I have ever known."

"My!" The queen sat back in her carriage. "Well, then. You have surprised me. Perhaps you are not what my son believed you to be."

Blythe let out a short chuckle. "Or maybe I have some more learning to do. Whatever the case, I am grateful Caspian came into my life because he taught me how to truly love someone from the inside out."

"Then I wish you luck! I wish you both luck." The queen grinned and then winked. "Do not forget to kiss him. And give him a kiss from me as well."

Baffled, Blythe stared at her.

Bethany giggled and then said cryptically, "I am sure we will be seeing each other soon. Farewell, Princess Blythe." And with that, she tapped upon the roof of the carriage with her cane and off it went.

Chapter Eighteen

BLYTHE WOULD NOT ALLOW herself much time to contemplate the words of Queen Bethany. Instead, she scoured the castle, looking for Caspian. She even went as far as to enlist the help of several maids and her sisters, but to no avail. He was simply not anywhere to be found.

After a couple of hours, she was worried and tired and so very confused. It must have been her. Something about her exchange with the two queens must have caused him to leave. But what? Was it so miserable here that he would wish to run away without another thought? Without even a good-bye?

If only she could pinpoint the problem, maybe she would be able to find the proper solution. She opened the door to her room and wiped at her eyes. It seemed they would be filled with silly tears for quite some time. She sighed and crossed to the looking glass, staring at the weary girl before her. One by one, she pulled the pins and ribbons from her hair, allowing it to fall in long waves to her waist.

She had so much hope that morning when she dressed in her village attire. And yet, now all that happiness and brightness was gone.

Blythe groaned and turned from the mirror, ready to throw herself across her bed, when there sleeping soundly upon a pink satin pillow was Caspian.

What?

"Caspian!" She ran to him, not caring if she woke him up. "Where have you been?"

He groggily opened an eye and smiled. "Hello to you too."

"None of your silliness now, sir!" she scolded. "I have been frantic with worry searching everywhere for you. I have even looked in this room a few times today and you were never found."

"I am sorry," he said as he stretched his limbs and sat up. "I was a fool."

"Where did you go?"

He glanced away and took a deep breath before his eyes met hers. "I left. I felt it was best if I did."

She leaned against the bed to help hold up her suddenly weak frame. "But why?"

"That does not matter as much as the motive for why I returned."

Not wishing to argue the point, for his reasons for leaving were very important to her, she asked, "And why was that?"

"Because after an hour or so of deep contemplation, I realized that no matter how harsh the reality of my life was at the moment, my heart could not bear to be without you."

All at once her breathing stopped. "What did you say?"

"I found the prospect of being alone much worse than being here with a woman who will never love me."

But it was not true! "Caspian, wait—"

He continued. "You have told me repeatedly what you think of me. You have even told my mother and celebrated the fact that we will never wed. I could not bear it another moment—I had to go. The idea of this transformation was to see if you were truly what I believed you to be. And instead, I found a stunning, kind, generous, adorable princess waiting to be loved. I could not help myself. I fell hopelessly and madly for a girl who will never wish to have anything to do with me."

Oh, my word. Nolan! He was Prince Nolan. "Can it be true? Are you my betrothed?"

He hung his head. "Yes."

"Prince Nolan!" She giggled, shocked and stunned. And then in the next instant, it hit her. "You have been Nolan all along!" She gasped and covered her mouth. "You have heard everything! I have allowed you to know everything. My thoughts, my dreams, my ..."

"Yes. Yes, I know."

"But ..." She shook her head. This could not be happening to her. Not now. Not when she had just decided she was in love with him.

"And the worst part, the part that eats me alive, is that while I misjudged you and thought you selfish and spoiled and all things horrid, yours was an act—a treatment of what I no doubt deserved. My assessment of you was false, but yours was undoubtedly correct in every aspect."

"No." She could not believe it. He was not that vain man, he was not—or he would not have cared for her as he did.

"Yes. And I know that while Caspian and Blythe have gotten along famously, I am afraid I am actually and will always be the foolhardy and arrogant Prince Nolan in your eyes."

She stared at him for a long moment, allowing all he had said to fully process. There were so many things she wished to convey, but first she needed to think. He left the drawing room because he was Prince Nolan. His mother's visit must have upset him greatly as well, which is why she behaved so oddly toward him and he toward her. He was attempting to stop her from revealing who he was because he did not want Blythe to know. He wanted to keep this a bit longer, this peace.

She blinked and took a deep breath.

He came back because he loved her as she loved him. He was not the man he believed he was. Any man who would risk his comforts

for a silly girl and turn himself into a frog
to truly get to know her character and then
fall in love with her goodness was not an
arrogant man. Indeed, this was a man who
acted on true character and principles of the
finest order. He might not know how to woo
a woman properly, but he could love. And he
could show love and make a girl feel as though
she belonged in ways she had never known.

What a farce this was! Blythe suddenly
giggled again. "To think that all this time,
I thought Prince Nolan was the enemy, and
he was not. He was the man I love." And
then, surprising even herself, she leaned over
and quickly kissed Caspian on the top of his
smooth froggy head.

"Blythe!" was all he said before a great
flash of bright yellow light exploded in her
room and nearly blinded her.

In fright, she ducked her head and then
when the light dissipated, she slowly raised
it to find the unbelievably handsome prince
sitting on her bed.

He was dressed to the hilt in his royal
green-and-gold Hollene court clothes.

Chapter Nineteen

PRINCE NOLAN GLANCED DOWN at
his princely form and let out a relieved sigh.
"Thank heavens! I am human again." He
looked up at her amazed features and grinned.
"Though I did enjoy riding upon your
shoulder. I may actually miss that."

Blythe continued to stare at him, her
mouth forming an enchanting O of surprise.

"Hello," he said. He had forgotten for
a moment that they had never actually met.
Though he knew her well, she was just now
seeing him in all his handsome glory for the
very first time. He attempted to smother
a chuckle. She really was one of the most

adorable women he had ever known, and her confusion at his looks only added to her charm.

Indeed, he was raised knowing how fortunate his striking face was. He knew the reactions of the courtiers and other princesses he had met—they each responded exactly as poor Blythe was now when in his presence for the first time.

He took after his father, who also had the same effect on women. It was this silliness that did make it rather hard for him to decide if they were truly interested or only pretended to be because of his looks.

He grinned and attempted to snap her out of her reverie as he moved a bit closer. "Princess Blythe," he said as he took her hand in his. "Please allow me to properly introduce myself." He brought her hand up and kissed the back. "I am Prince Nolan of Hollene Court, your intended, and I would like to honor that betrothal, if it would suit you as well."

All at once, Blythe came to. "Prince Nolan, you have precisely twenty seconds to remove yourself from my bed and room or I will throttle you!" She pulled her hand out of his.

"Wait. I know it is it because I am so good-looking. Just wait a moment and allow yourself to get used to my person."

Blythe's eyebrows rose. "Are you jesting?"

"You have been in a stupor for several seconds. I assumed it was because of how dashing I look."

"You *are* jesting. You must be, because no prince would say such a thing to the woman he hopes to marry one day. Now, out!" She pointed to the door. "Your time is up."

"What did I do?" he asked as he slipped off the bed.

"What did you do? What did you *do*?" Blythe began to push him out the door. "You have the idiocy to sit upon my bed and propose marriage to me as if we were in a brothel! And then tell me that my stunned looks at finding a full-grown man in my bed were most decidedly my confusion at your handsome face!"

Well, that would teach him to be so arrogant. He laughed as she shoved him out the door. Then he turned and grinned down at her glittering eyes. If looks could slay someone, her glare would have certainly destroyed him. "Where would you care to have my proposal of marriage, then?" he asked.

She groaned and closed those eyes. "Do not look at me like that. You will make me smile, and I refuse to smile when I am attempting to stay mad at you."

"Forgive me for monstrously ruining my first attempt at a proposal and making you feel as if you were in a brothel. Now, where would you prefer to hear my words of agreement toward you? For you must know, I find you to be exceedingly more dear than any girl I have ever met. However, if I have just now ruined your hopes of finding me less vain than you believed, I will do everything in my power to attempt to grow and become a better man so that I may win your heart."

She shook her head. "Nolan, no." She chuckled then. "I mean, yes, you did ruin that quite atrociously. But I can easily forgive you for your momentary lapse of common sense. You do not need to grow more—I find you magnificent just the way you are. Indeed, I must be the one to apologize to you, for it is I who judged you wrongly from the beginning. And I would have most likely continued to judge you had you not come as you did and allowed me to get to know your soul."

It was so marvelous to be able to stand at his full height and to see her so very close and so very charming. "Blythe?"

"Yes?"

"I will declare myself properly by the pond where we met—your most favorite place in the world. But if I do not express my love and hope for a future with you right now, I feel as though my heart might burst. I love you." He reached out and finally ran his hand through her silken hair, cupping her head. How many times had he wished to do this? Tugging her gently closer, he whispered, "You care about so very many things. You laugh, you banter, you can hold your own in any argument, and your soul is sweeter than any I have ever known."

His gaze caressed her perfect features as he wrapped an arm around her waist. "I desire more than anything to express my ardent wish to make you mine, though I am afraid to hear your words lest you reject me. I have been a fool for too long. Thank you for teaching me how to truly treat a woman."

"I will only accept your proposals at the pond if you kiss me this instant."

"Hush, minx." Nolan laughed, his whole chest warm from the glow in her eyes. "I do believe you shall keep me on my toes for an eternity."

"I would hope so." She brazenly placed her arms about his neck. "For I know of no one I would prefer to spend my eternity with."

How could he deny her another moment? Nolan swiftly pulled her in and kissed her soft lips for some time until she moaned and pulled back.

"My goodness! I would have kissed you much earlier if I had known this was to be my reward!"

Grinning, he brought her in and properly silenced any more wayward silliness from her until she melted into him.

Chapter Twenty

A LITTLE WHILE LATER, after sneaking out of the castle so they would not alarm anyone with the sight of the transformed prince, Blythe traveled hand in hand with Nolan to the pond. It did not take him long to kneel upon one knee and properly ask for her heart to be his always. Once done, she happily snuggled up with her new fiancé upon her boulder.

"Blythe, I have been thinking," he said. "What if we include monies to provide for a schoolteacher for your kingdom as a part of the marriage settlement between me and your mother? Do you think that would work?"

She sat up and pulled back to see him

better. "Do you really mean that?"

"Of course. I cannot simply take you away and abandon the children without their education."

"Oh, Nolan! You are too good. I have been so worried about leaving them, I did not know what I would do."

"Well, this seems like the perfect opportunity to correct the state of your kingdom, then. For if I have it decreed, in exchange for your hand, the continual funding necessary to pay for the new teacher and schooling, I do not see how she can resist, or how she can put up a fuss over such things. If Prince Nolan of Hollene finds it essential, how could Queen Mary not?"

"Precisely! You are a genius. For she could turn me away, but could she turn away such a wealthy and handsome prince?" Blythe grinned.

"Why do I feel as though you are gently mocking me?"

She shrugged. "I most likely am, but it does not signify. I do believe my mother will go along with whatever you ask of her. Especially something like this, that does not take any time or effort or even money on her part." She suddenly kissed him. "Thank you. Thank you for thinking of those children. How blessed they are! How blessed I am to have you in my life. I love you."

"No, my dear, it is I who is blessed. I have and will always be blessed for knowing you and finding such a dear, sweet woman to attach myself to." He kissed her again and then pulled back. "However, I guess perhaps a little of the credit should go to our mothers, too."

"Oh goodness, yes!" She chuckled. "That is, if we have not ruined everything after today."

"My mother will not care overly much. I know—I was waiting in the carriage. I figured it would be the easiest way to get home. But I spoke with her before I came back inside your castle."

"Did you?"

"Yes, it was my mother who convinced me to stay in the end. I think she saw how much I loved you."

"Before she drove away, she asked me what I thought of the frog. And I answered truthfully, that I have never loved anyone more." She looked at his lips. "Which reminds me, I have a kiss to give you from her."

"A kiss?"

"I thought it was an odd request at the time, but then again, I had not realized who you were yet." She leaned up and kissed him. "Despite her revealing what you thought of me, I do think I will like her very much."

"And even if you did not, it is fine. Because you will always have me to love." He kissed her again.

"Or pummel you."

"There is that. However, you can only pummel me when I need a good thump and have done something excessively outrageous."

"Like propose to me upon my bed?"

"Yes, exactly so."

"Prince Nolan of Hollene Court, I will never willingly harm you, for you truly love me. All of our arguments and frustrations will be just that—arguments and frustrations. For I have the security deep down that we will always have one another once those angry feelings wane, and I am reminded of the goodness of your heart and your true character once again." She grinned. "I cannot wait to finally begin my life with you. Thank you for seeing me."

"No." He shook his head. "Thank you for seeing *me*. Not very many women would have, nor would they have treated a frog as nicely as you did."

"You started it. You were kind enough to collect my ball for me."

"Then may we have a lifetime of kindness between us both."

"Yes, let us do so. It sounds like heaven to me."

And it was. Prince Nolan and Princess Blythe wed just three months later in a simple ceremony to the happiness and delight of both kingdoms. They went on to have two adorable little girls who loved to play with slimy frogs and swim in dirty ponds, to the great chagrin of their poor governess and maids.

Queen Mary Elizabeth II and Queen Bethany were able to resolve their differences, and with the addition of their granddaughters, they soon became the best of friends again and had many opportunities to take the little girls on adventures.

Nolan was true to his word and not only made sure that Blythe's kingdom had the funding necessary for a teacher, but that Hollene received one as well. He was always heard to say that none of the teachers who had been hired were as good as Blythe.

Blythe still taught when she could, but for the most part stayed busy within her own castle. She and Nolan were often planning some big feast or party or celebration—anything to bring joy to their people, for they were determined to see their kingdom as happy as they were.

And they did. But how could they not? For this truly is a tale of a prince and princess who learned that the worth of the soul is so much greater than what is first perceived. Equality and love for all became the founding basis for their kingdom, and they learned to live by that quite nicely. So much so, they all lived happily ever after.

THE END

Preview of

The Twelve
Dancing Princesses

Chapter One

"HELLO!"

Aleck looked up from snipping at the ornamental hedges in the palace garden to see Princess Cascadia coming toward him. He immediately dropped his shears and lowered into a bow. "Your Highness," he said as he came back up to face the pretty dark-haired young woman. She looked exceptionally fetching today in a pale blue gown and matching ribbons.

She smiled and then stopped right in front of him. "Hello," she said again, as she slowly twirled the white lace parasol behind her head.

He waited a moment for her to say

something while his stomach did flip-flops. How many days had he watched the beautiful princess and wished for opportunities like this to speak with her? And yet, when they came, he had nothing to say. How does a simple gardener go about speaking with royalty?

She continued to twirl and wait, her grin growing.

Say something, you dolt! He swallowed nervously and then asked, "Would you like a flower?"

"A flower?" She looked at the hedge he had been pruning.

"No. Not from here." He pointed out behind him. "We could pick one from the queen's garden, if you would like. I know of some lovely daffodils that have just bloomed."

"Oh! Yes, please."

"If you follow me, I will show you just where they are." He began to walk, and then when he noticed she was not with him, he turned around. Princess Cascadia stood in the exact same spot. Confused, he asked, "Would you rather I went without you and brought back a couple?"

She shook her head. "No."

Good heavens, how was a man supposed to know what it is that women want? "Then you would not like to follow me?"

She chuckled, her laugh floating about her like tinkling fairy bells. "No, Aleck. I wish for you to lend me your arm so that we may go together."

How could he be so thoughtless? "Of course." He rushed to her side. "Forgive me." Being so close to her, close enough to smell the lavender soap she used, caused his breathing to become quite erratic. He glanced down at her side and then slowly offered his arm, willing himself to act natural as she daintily placed the top of her gloved hand upon his. He gazed into those sky-blue eyes a moment, reminding himself to breathe.

He was holding her arm. Her hand upon his. Her waist a mere inches from him. They were together—truly together—for the first time. A warmth spread through him he had never known before, sending a concentrated group of tingles at their touching limbs. He grinned at her and then watched in amazement as she inhaled sharply.

This overwhelming feeling affected her as

well! She could feel it.

Those eyes sparkled back at him. He was lost. Truly and foolishly lost.

Could she possibly think of him as he thought of her? Could the princess actually wish to be with a mere gardener?

A dog barked some distance away and snapped him back to the present. "Come, and we shall find the most enchanting daffodils for you."

He took a step forward, and then another, half expecting her to turn around and run the other way, but she did not. Instead she quite happily followed him.

Nothing had ever felt more right and wonderful than this moment.

"Aleck?" she asked as they slowly made their way to the flower garden.

"Yes?"

"I know this is highly improper and I will most likely get scolded if I am to be caught walking with you, but thank you for doing so."

His gaze met hers again. "It is my pleasure."

She nodded and glanced away, a faint blush stealing across her cheeks. All at once, the parasol began to twirl twice as fast as it had before. "Sir, you flatter me."

"I do not mean to flatter, Princess," he said with a grin, loving this new game of theirs. "Indeed, I only mean to speak the absolute truth. This is by far the most pleasurable moment of my day."

She gasped and glanced his way before biting her lip and looking away again.

He could not believe his eyes. If he did not know better, she would seem to be genuine in her response to him. "Why did you ask to hold my arm?" he brazenly asked, curious as to how she would reply.

She kept her profile to him as they continued to walk. "Because I knew you would never think to offer, and so I asked for myself."

"Because?"

"Because I wanted to," she replied.

"Fair enough." He let the subject drop. "And have you had any news to impart? Any reason for us to be thus engaged?"

"News?"

"Yes. For when your mother asks why you have been traipsing the grounds with a lowly gardener, you will have a much better reply to give her than because you wanted to."

She blushed again and then shook her head. "You are incorrigible."

"I know. I think it is why you like me." He said the last looking straight at her again.

She gasped in shock. "I have said no such thing!"

He stopped, his back toward the many windows of the castle, stepping forward and hiding her for a brief moment. "You did not have to say anything to me. I can tell by your actions." His heart grew a bit heavier. "Princess, as much as I wish to keep you near me to learn every possible secret of yours and gain your trust, I fear for this."

"I have come outside every single day for the past several months in hopes of …" She trailed off.

Speaking with me. "Aye. I think I understand, but it will not do. I am merely a gardener. And as much as you would be scolded for doing such a thing, I would be dismissed from my post completely if this were to continue."

"No." Her breathing became labored. She

truly looked distraught over this declaration.

Did she honestly have no idea that such things were frowned upon? "What is it?"

"-Tis not fair," she said after a few moments. "I—I do not know how to express myself, or why. It does not make sense to me. But there is something about you that calls to me. Something I cannot dismiss."

She *did* feel it too! He clutched her hand. "Princess Cascadia!"

"Please, call me Casey. I have abhorred that name my whole life. Casey is what I prefer."

"I cannot. I do not dare. You know the help is not allowed to speak so casually of you," he whispered as he glanced around, making certain they were alone.

She squeezed his fingers. "Please?"

How could he deny her anything? He took a deep breath.

"Please?"

"Casey," he said. The name was so profound, it was as if it echoed between them for several seconds.

And then she smiled. Truly, her whole face lit up. "Thank you."

At that moment he saw the head gardener walking toward them. "Give me a reason to be standing here with you. Tell me something important so that I may continue working here."

Her eyes frantically searched his before they lit up and she said, "I have it! There is a great secret happening in the house. And who knows, perhaps you will be the one to solve the mystery." She grinned. "Yes! Father is to send out a proclamation within a week asking for brave men to solve the puzzle of me and my sisters' dancing slippers."

He blinked. "Your what?"

"Every morning when we awake, our shoes are completely worn through, as if we have been dancing all night. But none of us can remember leaving our beds. Indeed, it is frightening to see the state of the slippers. And our feet! Sometimes they are swollen and blistered as well. And yet, we were asleep."

"This happens to all twelve of you?"

"Yes. Oh!" She laughed out loud, causing the head gardener to speed up his walking toward them. "It is perfect!" she said, clasping his hand tighter. "Father said that whoever is able to solve the mystery will be allowed to choose one of his daughters to wed!"

Aleck felt as though he had been punched in the chest. My word! Could it be true? Could this be actually happening to him? Was there a way to have this angel by his side permanently?

"Aleck? Aleck? Are you well?"

He glanced at her. "I believe so."

"Then will you try to solve the riddle?"

The gardener glared at him, but remained silent as he passed the princess. Aleck knew this would be horrendous for them both. His eyes searched Casey's and he nodded. "Yes, I will try my best to solve the mystery of the dancing princesses."

ABOUT THE AUTHOR

JENNI JAMES IS THE busy mom of seven rambunctious children ranging from the ages of 2-16. When she isn't chasing them around her house in sunny New Mexico, she is dreaming of new books to write. She loves to hear from her readers and can be contacted at:

jenni@authorjennijames.com,
or by writing to:

Jenni James
PO Box 514
Farmington, NM 87499

Printed in Great Britain
by Amazon